Review

Raleigh Minard's novel *Billy Webber and the Sky Pirates* is an entertaining anachronism. Adventure stories like this are uncommon in the twenty-first century and recall and bygone era when the young relished stories featuring daredevil heroes prevailing over fearsome foes and impossible odds. Minard structures the novel around an old man recalling his friendship with Webber when they were young, but there are problems with the execution. Grandpa Collins relates experiences he couldn't have possibly witnessed, but this drawback is small and isn't a fatal flaw.

The dialogue is one of the novel's strongest attributes. Minard's exchanges develop character and advance the plot without extended monologues and contrast well with his descriptive powers. He excels with the book's action sequences thanks to his unwillingness to let things turn overwrought and the interplay between various characters has ample credibility. *Billy Webber and the Sky Pirates,* in some ways, might make a more effective screenplay than novel thanks to the dialogue and imaginative conceptual foundation driving the book forward.

The mix of fantasy and science fiction conceits works better than you might expect. An important reason for this is because Minard keeps his fictional landscape grounded in convincing reality with his strong characterizations. The characters inhabit a fantastic, yet familiar, world yet never treat it as such. The book moves at an entertaining pace, but readers will never feel like Minard glosses over critical plot points.

Minard is not a novice writer. It is obvious from the outset the author began this book with a clear idea of how to develop the story, the characters, and where the story is going. There is no hesitation. The confidence on display throughout the entirety of *Billy Webber and the Sky Pirates* is one of its highlights and carries readers through the book, negating its minor flaws, and compelling you to keep moving forward with the novel. This is no small thing.

It builds to an impressive conclusion. One of the most impressive aspects of the ending is its unpredictability and the creativity fueling the novel spills over into the memorable climax without ever seeming forced. Minard ties up the various plot strands in a believable fashion and his skill at never straining readers' suspension of disbelief is key to the book's success. Minard draws you into the novel's fictional landscape with ease and the book's length never taxes your attention. *Billy Webber and the Sky Pirates* is a book you can devour in a single sitting and likely holds up under repeated readings.

It will appeal to a wide age range. The novel will grip young men and women swooning with their first love for reading books while older readers will find *Billy Webber and the Sky Pirates* transports them to another fully realized world providing them much needed escape from the day's cares and worries. Raleigh Minard's book will hit the sweet spot for many readers and establishes an imaginative world begging further exploration. Let's hope we hear more from this author soon.

- Jason Hillenburg, Reprospace Reviews™

Billy
WEBBER
And The Sky Pirates

RALEIGH MINARD

Billy Webber and The Sky Pirates
First edition, published 2020

By Raleigh Minard

Copyright © 2020, Raleigh Minard

Cover design by Reprospace.com

Paperback ISBN-13: 978-1-952685-09-5

Published by Kitsap Publishing
Poulsbo, WA 98370
www.KitsapPublishing.com

To my Lord for
inspiration and help.

To Bobbie Kuniyuki,
for being honest with me.

Prologue

Our story begins on a world so far away; its light has yet to reach the Sol solar system. The name of the world is for lack of a better translation is called Topaz. The world of Topaz doesn't have super landmasses; they have only a couple of large islands just half the size of our Australia and many smaller islands, some not even explored yet. The oceans are of freshwater, and the Islands where people live, you'd believe that you could transplant people from our earth from the 1930s, and they'd seem to be right at home. The shape of the cars, trains, planes, and the buildings. Even the way people dressed. Now the people would also give away the fact that this was not earth. The people were shorter than us, and the had an appearance much like elves with pointed ears, their hair had the same range of color as we do except for the purple, green tints around the edges. Beyond that, they were people much like our selves. Now on with our story about Billy Webber and the Sky Pirates.

Chapter

1
___

"Come on kids; we're going to go see Grandpa Collins."

"Oh, Dad, do we have to?" asks Jeff.

"Jeff, you love grandpa's stories; why don't you want to go?"

"Yea, but they're always the same stories."

"That maybe, but one minute into the story, you're always lost in the adventure grandpa spins."

"I guess so," said Jeff as he kicks at the ground.

"Today, we're all going to listen; I want to record these stories so I can write a book."

"Why, dad? Who'll read them?"

"Well, son, lots of people will read them, some for entertainment, and others for history."

"History?" asks Jeff.

"Yes, Jeff. History. Grandfather lived what he talks about in his stories. Grandpa also was a friend to William (Billy) Webber."

"You mean these aren't just made up stories?"

"Not at all. Go to the library and look up William Webber. You'll find photographs of grandpa and Billy Webber together."

"Grandpa knew Billy Webber?"

"I knew Billy Webber too. He lived with us when I was young.

"What are we waiting for dad, let's go to grandpas."

The whole family piled into the family velocipede, and an hour later, they arrive at grandpa's (John Collins) house. Jeff is the first one out of the velocipede.

"Grandpa, grandpa, I heard you were friends with Billy Webber. Is that true?"

"Well, sport it's true, but I was more like his father, but I'll tell you more after your dad sets up his recorder."

Doug Collins sets up his recorder and tells Jeff to be very quiet, questions are ok, but no rough-housing while Grandpa Collins is telling his story.

Grandpa Collins looks up at the sky as he contemplates where to start, with his hand on his chin and then he looks down at his audience, Jeff and his younger sister are sitting on the patio floor, and mom and dad are at the table. Everyone is anxious to hear grandpa's story.

"Let me see; when I first meet Billy over forty years ago, his father had been killed recently in a battle with the Sky Pirates. You see Billy's father was a great pilot, as I recall. He was on a secret mission to get information on the Sky Pirates. He was discovered and tried to escape and get the information back to his command. He was shot down and killed before he could getaway. Billy started nursing a hatred for the Sky

Pirates. It was not long until Billy started showing up at the airfield. Billy was about six years old at that time, and he was full of questions. I guess most young boys usually are. Billy would come down to the airfield and watch the planes land and take off, that's when I first saw him. I walked over to him and asked him what he was doing there, and his reply was just watching. I told Billy to stay where he was and stay out of trouble, and he could watch. True to his word, he stayed put." grandpa paused for a moment as if he was trying to organize his thoughts, and he took a drink of his ice-cold tea.

"Now, where were we? Oh, yes, I remember. One day I looked out to see Billy was at the fence; then, I saw a woman approach him. It turned out to be his mother. I walked over to make sure everything was all right. I stopped dead in my tracks. She was scolding Billy quite sternly. As it turns out, she didn't want Billy there watching the planes. She was afraid Billy would want to become a flier, like his father, so she made excuses about how dangerous it was to hang out there. I stepped in to rescue Billy. Hello Mrs. Webber, I'm Jim Collins, and I've been keeping an eye on Billy to make sure he stays out of trouble."

"Thank you, Mr. Collins, but I don't want Billy causing any problems here."

"Mam, would it be ok if Billy came to work for me, sweeping up the hangar, picking up loose trash, and I'd keep an eye on him."

I could see she was struggling with the decision, I learned later she didn't want Billy to be a flier, but Mrs. Webber gave in after seeing the look of disappointment in Billy's eyes.

"She agreed to let Billy work in my hangar, but only if he stayed away from the landing strip."

"Billy had a job working for me, he was a good lad, on the first day Billy sweeps the hangar floor, you could see the concrete, at lunchtime I noticed he didn't have one so I shared mine with him. All he wanted to do was talk about planes and flying. I'd answer one question; then, ten more questions would pop out. I guess all us boys were like that. So, I tried to answer his questions, and some of them I couldn't.

Time went by, and Billy started school, he was a good student. He realized that if he wanted to be a flyer and an aircraft mechanic, he'd need to know how to read, write, and do numbers. Billy consumed learning like a hungry man looking for food. Over time, Billy's questions grew more and more around aircraft, and I did my best to answer them, then one day I took him to the library and showed him how to look things up. It wasn't long, and it seemed he read all the books on airplanes. One Saturday, Billy was working the back lot to get rid of the junk I had out there.

Before I knew it, it's all cleaned up, and the yard is nearly spotless. That day I walked Billy over to the cafeteria in the terminal and bought him lunch and let him sit next to the window so he could watch the planes land and take off. Billy was so enthralled he almost didn't eat his lunch. I decided to have Billy help me work on the aircraft that came to my hangar. By this time, Billy was ten years old and was about as tall as he was going to get. Billy was a small man, his head came up to my chin, his hair was very curly, and a tan color.

Billy had violet-colored eyes. I had decided to have Billy help me rebuild one of the engines. The first time it took a Big longer to rebuild, so I could teach Billy how to do it right. The next rebuild went faster. Billy was a quick study, and soon he could tear down an engine and rebuild it in a few days.

Soon we moved on to the rest of the plane, doing the wings, fuselage, landing gear, and so on. The last thing I taught Billy was how to use the crystal components. For most planes, the crystals powered the engines of all our vehicles, and like everything else, Billy bought or borrowed books on rebuilding aircraft. By the time he reached eighteen, he would be as knowledgeable as any full-blown mechanic. Then tragedy struck Billy again. I remember it was a dreary wet day; a Policeman came to the hangar looking for Billy.

"What is it officer, what happened?"

"The officer told me what happened; it appeared that the Sky Pirates attacked a bank in broad daylight and robbed it. The police were moving in to catch them when they open fire on the people on the street, and Mrs. Webber was killed. The policeman came here to tell him and take him to the station."

"Officer, let me tell him, and I'll take him home with me."

"Are you sure you want to do that?" the police officer asked.

"Not really, but it'd be kinder coming from me than from you."

"Ok, but you'll need to bring him down to the station tomorrow."

"I'll bring him."

It was the hardest thing I had ever had to do. How do you

tell an eighteen your old boy his mother was killed? I walked over to the cafeteria where Billy was eating his lunch and sat down beside him, and my face must have been very long, Billy picked up right away that something was wrong.

"Jim, what's wrong?"

I was almost in tears. "Billy, a policeman, was there looking for you, he wanted to tell you that your mother was killed, during a bank robbery, and the police want to talk with you tomorrow. I said I'd bring you with me."

"Nooo! Not my mother. Who's responsible?"

"The police will tell you tomorrow, Billy; I'm so sorry for you." I put my hand on his shoulder while he cried. It was breaking my heart, sitting there, not knowing what to do. That night I took him to my house to spend the night. After dinner, I talked to my wife about Billy staying with us. She said, no! She had not told me yet that she was carrying our first child, and she saw that I cared for Billy, and I might not pay attention to our child if he was here. Billy heard our conversation and stayed the night. The next morning, we went to the police station, and Billy answered all the questions put to him. During the questioning, Billy found out that, the Sky Pirates had killed his mother. This increased Billy's resolve to destroy them.

The police were going to place Billy in protective custody, mostly to keep him from doing what he was planning to do. Go after the Sky Pirates. I stepped up and asked if he could stay with me; they thought it over and let me take him home. I spent the day with Billy at the hangar, and at the end of the day, Billy ran away. He left me a note. "Your wife is concerned about me, causing you trouble, and that may be true, so I'll go home and pick up my stuff and find a place of my own. I'll be back in the morning to help with work. That should keep me out of trouble with you and the law."

The kid has sand, he kept his word, it took a while, but I found out where Billy was living. There was an old hangar on the edge of the flight field, and in one of the back-rooms was an office with a bathroom where Billy made his home. I checked with the airport manager and found out the hangar was for sale at a meager price. I purchased it and talked to Billy when he came to work the next day.

"Billy, I just bought the hangar at the edge of the field, and I know you live there. I'll sell it to you for the price I paid for it."

"Thanks, Jim. I'll pay you back." Billy started to rebuild his new home and hangar, this allowed him to open his own business of rebuilding aircraft. Instead of competing with me, he helped me by taking my overflow of work. We both made out well. In the first year, Billy paid for his hangar. Then he started putting his money towards repairing more of his hangar. While he was working on it, an airplane crashed, coming in for a landing. Everyone ran out to see if anyone was hurt and to provide help if necessary. They dragged the aircraft off the field so it could let other planes land or takeoff. All the people on the crashed plane were ok, but the plane was damaged beyond repair. Billy talked to the owner to see if he could have the aircraft. The owner was responsible for having the craft removed at his expense. So, he decided to give it to Billy.

Billy towed the aircraft to his hangar and placed it in the far corner, where he could tear it down and salvage the good parts. Billy decided to get rid of the too severely damaged components. The engine was toast and most of the fuselage, but the crystals that drive the plane were still intact, and a lot of the hardware was salvageable, along with the electronics. Billy kept the crystals and sold the equipment after he checked them out. Billy scraped the airplane and sold it to a scrap yard, and the components to a second-hand dealer. Then Billy got inspired to build his own plane. Billy decided to make what we call a Bee Gee; it is a tail dragger type plane small and fast. They're used in flying races.

Chapter

2

Billy has the crystals, and by selling the parts from the crashed plane, he starts looking for a Bee Gee plane kit. He knows enough to be able to put one together. Billy shops around and finds an old Bee Gee for sale. He gets me to take him to see the plane. The plane was in such lousy shape Billy rejects it. Billy keeps looking until he finds a kit that someone ordered then changed his mind. Billy was able to convince the seller to sell it at a discount. Billy now has a plane but no motor. That'll have to come later, but in the meantime, Billy can start building his plane. One day I walk over to Billy's hangar to see how he's doing, and he's about halfway through building his new Bee Gee plane.

"Billy, I see you're coming along very well on your plane; have you given any thought about flying lessons. After all, you'll want to fly this crate when you have it finished."

"No Jim, I hadn't thought about it, I was concentrating so hard on building my plane I didn't think about the flying part, and you're right I'll want to fly as soon as it's built."

"Come with me. I'll introduce you to a friend of mine and your father's; he's an outstanding pilot."

Billy drops what he's doing and follows Jim over to the cafeteria, and in one corner, Jim directs Billy over to this older man who was drinking coffee. Jim sits down and waves Billy over to sit with him.

"Billy, this Dave Johnson, he taught your father to fly."

"You both knew my father?"

Dave spoke up. "Yes, I knew your father, he was my best student, and he could outfly anyone. He even outdid the most dangerous Sky Pirate of the time. It was tough luck that a whole squadron of pirates caught him alone and brought him down."

"I hear from Jim here that you want to take flying lessons."

"That's right I do, how much will it cost?"

"That depends on how well you fly. If you've the talent like your father, it'll cost you nothing. On the other hand, if you fly like most of these jokers, a hundred dollars a session."

"When can we start?"

"Tomorrow, too late?"

"No, Sir, that'll be fine. Where and when?"

"Tomorrow morning at Sun up right here. If you're late, that'll tell me you don't want to learn, and I'll go on my way. You see, kid, I don't do much teaching anymore. When I learned who your father was, I decided to teach one more student. Don't disappoint me."

Dave gets up and looks deep into Billy's eyes, and then he reaches over to Jim and shakes his hand. Then he turns and walks away.

"Well, Billy, that was very encouraging."

"What do you mean?"

"He looked you in the eyes; he sees something there."

"What does he see?"

"What he saw in your father's eyes all those years ago. Determination."

Jim leads Billy out of the building.

"Dave is a funny person Billy, pay him respect and never be late. If you're late even one time, he'll stop teaching you. Most of all, take it seriously."

"Whatever you say, Jim."

The next morning Dave is waiting at the cafeteria before Sun up, and mere moments later, Billy is there. Dave hands Billy a packet of materials consisting of maps, flight-computer the manual type, and then a flight manual. At last, Dave gives Billy an old pouch to keep them in.

"Today, we'll go over what you need to know to navigate, then we'll walk around my plane to do some hands-on preflight, and I'll take us up for a short hop."

Billy's response, for the time being, is "Yes Sir!"

Dave gives Billy his first lecture on how to use the maps and the manual flight-computer for navigation. Then Dave leads the way out to his trainer, which is much like a piper cub with two seats.

"Being the mechanic Jim says you are, we're going to go over the parts of the aircraft things like wings, rudder, elevators, and the flight controls. If you feel like you are being treated like a kid, you are. Now any questions?"

"When might I be able to fly?"

"Billy, that'll be determined by how well you follow instruction. Now tell me what you know of this aircraft."

Billy correctly identifies all the parts of the aircraft and how they function. Dave has Billy get into the pilot's seat, and he takes the trainer's position. Dave fires up the plane and taxis out on to the tarmac then calls the tower. Soon Dave is racing down the runway and lifts off into the air. Once Dave is high enough, he does a series of rolls, and dives, the whole time he is watching Billy, the more stunts Dave did, the more excited Billy became.

"Billy, take the stick."

Billy grabs the stick, and Dave walks him around on how to make the plane move and climb. A right turn, and left turn, then a dive. Then Dave asks for the stick back, and Billy lets Dave take it.

"How did I do, Dave?"

"Better than I expected Billy, I'll be here tomorrow; I'm going to give you a quiz to see if you are paying attention."

Dave lands the plane, taxis to Jim's hangar, and parks the aircraft. Billy gets out and ties the aircraft down.

Dave walks into Jim's hangar, while Billy heads for his hanger to get in some study time.

"Dave, how did Billy do?"

"He is going to be a better pilot than his father, matter of fact; he is going to be one of the greatest pilots that I've ever taught. He handled that plane up there as if he were born in. I'll know better tomorrow after my Quiz and another flight test."

Early the next morning, Billy was waiting for Dave to show

up. It was moments later when Dave appears. They went inside the cafeteria and ordered coffee and retired to the back of the room. Dave gave Billy his navigation test to work on and walked away. Dave thought he had plenty of time to order his breakfast and eat before Billy could finish the test. Just as Dave's food was placed on the counter and before Dave could sample the food, Billy was standing beside him.

"What do you have a question on the test?" asked Dave.

Billy looks at him and says, "No question, I've completed the test you gave me."

Dave looked disappointed, so he took the test and started reading it, and then he looks up at Billy.

"No one has ever finished this test that quickly, how'd you do it so quickly?" exclaimed Dave.

"I studied all night, and then I saw how easy it was to do, I did most of the calculations in my head, it wasn't very hard."

Dave looked at Billy, "Empty your pockets."

Billy complied; Billy even turned out the old binder that Dave gave him. Then as a last resort, Dave got up and checked the garbage pales, which were all empty. In shock, Dave sat down and ate his breakfast, and then he ordered one for Billy. All Dave said during the whole meal is, "I don't believe it." Then Dave would look at Billy and shake his head. After they ate, they went out to the piper cub, and Dave told Billy to preflight the plane. Billy did it right the first time out. Billy even checked some of the items seldom inspected by most pilots.

Dave is astounded at how fast Billy learns. They get into the plane, and Dave has Billy take off. Then do some of the same stunts they did the day before, and then Dave has Billy land the plane. Dave is beside himself.

"Billy, I've never trained anyone like you in my entire life, where I show you one time, and you pick it right away. You read a book and pick up the concept. I've a few other things I want to show you. Right now, I have to go wrap my head around what you did today." He mumbled in disbelief to himself.

Billy ties the aircraft down and watches Dave walk into Jim's Hangar, just shaking his head. Dave runs into Jim.

"Well, Dave, how is Billy doing?"

"I've never had a student do what Billy has done. He completed my test in one hour. Never has anyone done that in my whole life, He took up the plane and landed it today. No one has ever taken a plane up the second time and flown without any help."

"Dave, are you going to teach him?"

"Are you kidding next month he'll be teaching me? Yes, by all that is good, Billy is going to be the greatest pilot this world has ever seen."

"That is great, Dave. I think we should help him, don't you?"

"What do you have in mind, Jim?"

"Dave, you and I are going to buy Billy a motor for his Bee Gee. What do you say to that?"

"You're on, I've never seen a flyer like this kid, and the sooner we get him in the air, the better."

Two days later, a truck pulls up to Billy's hangar and drops off an engine for the Bee Gee. Billy walks out of the hangar.

"Hey! What's going on here?"

"Are you Billy Webber?"

"Yes."

"Sign here, please."

"I didn't order this engine."

"You are Billy Webber, are you not?"

"Yes."

"Then the engine gets dropped off here, what you do with it after that is your problem."

The delivery van then drives away. Jim saw the delivery and walks over with a puzzled look on his face.

"What is going on, Billy?"

"Did you get this engine for me?"

"Not really, Wow it's a nice one, looks like it needs a Big work, I bet it'll fit into your Bee Gee."

"If you didn't get it for me, who did?"

"As the master says, everything comes to all who wait."

"Well, Jim, since you're here, help me push this thing into the hangar."

Billy is beside himself about the new engine, but he has a flight test in the morning, so he goes to his room and pours a cup of coffee and studies for his flight-test. Billy turns in early and then gets up early excited after today he'll be certified to fly. Billy meets with Dave for his last test. Billy aces the written part, then he has to fly the Piper Cub by himself, and he has to fly to two different cities and back here to complete his test all in twenty-four hours. Billy takes off and does the first leg of his flight-test in record time, with the wind at his back. The second leg of the flight was a bit slower, fighting a crosswind, costing Billy some extra time. After Billy lands at the second city, the headwinds pick up, and he'll not make it in the twenty-four-hour window. Billy Pulls out his maps and calculator, and as he looks over the flight plan, Billy sees that if he can fly through the canyon that runs in the same direction, he might just make it with some time to spare. Billy fires up the plane and heads for the canyon. This canyon is much like our Grand Canyon, but a few places in this canyon are close enough to jump from one side to the other.

Billy fights the headwind to the end of the canyon. And Billy drops down into it and notices the speed of the plane has increased since the wind is now going overhead, and he's down inside the canyon. Billy dodges the spires within the canyon, and in one of the spots where the canyon top nearly comes to gather, Billy drops lower and flies through the eye of the needle. Soon Billy makes up his time, but he continues to operate in the canyon until he reaches the nearest point of departure for his final leg. An hour later, he sees the landing field and lands the Pipe Cub; when Billy lands, no one is there to meet him. Billy notes the time in the terminal and has the office man note it on his logbook.

Billy walks into the cafe, and everyone is listening to the radio.

"Hi, Dave, what's going on?"

Dave, without looking up to see who spoke. "Some crazy fool is flying the canyon, and right now, they're not sure if he has made it or crashed. No one has ever flown the canyon and survived to tell about it."

"Oh, Then I guess I'll be the first."

Dave and Jim looked up.

"Billy, that fool was you!" said Dave.

"Yea, I guess so, what's the problem?"

"No one has ever flown the canyon and lived to tell about it, threading the needle has always killed the people trying to fly through it," said Dave.

"Well, Dave, there is not a scratch on your Piper, and I flew the canyon. Otherwise, I'd still be trying to get here. The headwind was too strong, so I picked what I thought to be a path of least resistance."

When it sunk into everyone's mind, what Billy just accomplished, it became an instant party. One thing Billy can't do any better than anyone else is holding his booze. The next morning Billy wakes up in his bed, with his clothes on, smelling like booze and like someone threw upon him. Billy crawled into the bathroom, and every Big noise made him cringe and hold his head.

"I don't think I'm ever going to do that again," mumbled Billy.

After getting dressed, Billy stumbles out of the hangar and heads to the cafeteria to get some coffee. Billy felt like he was going to die, and somehow, he wished he could. Jim came in not long after and walked up to Billy. Jim pats Billy on the shoulder and tells him good morning with a smile. Billy wanted to kill me; I could see that right away.

"I didn't tell Billy I was in the same shape; I managed to bluff my way through the day."

That evening Dave felt well enough to come to the field to inspect his plane and then look up Billy to give him the news that he passed the test with excellence. Dave presented Billy with his license and other documents. That night Jim asked Billy if he'd do him a favor. Jim had booked a restaurant and dancing for his wife's birthday, but the baby sitter got sick, and would Billy please sit with the baby tonight.

"I know nothing about babies, other than they are wet at both ends and cry a lot."

"That's Ok, my wife has leftover dinner from last night, and her Stew is the best you can get. Also, she'll show you how to change the diapers and feed Big Doug."

"Ok, Jim, I'll do it, after all the things you did for me, I can tough it out for one night."

Jim Takes Billy to his home and the wife does have dinner all ready, and she is all dolled up. She takes Billy to the kitchen and shows him where the bottle is and how to warm it up, then on to the bedroom, where she instructs him on how to change a diaper. Billy is somewhat less than thrilled about changing a dirty diaper. Soon the two are off to dinner and dancing. Billy finished his dinner. He had to admit it was delicious. Soon the baby is crying, so Billy checks him out, and the diaper is still dry, and Billy has strict instructions when to feed the baby, and it was not for a while yet. Billy picks up the baby, and he quiets down. When Billy puts the baby back to bed, he starts crying again.

Billy decides to take the baby out to the front room and sit in a comfortable chair and rock him, soon Doug is sound asleep. Billy soon follows suit, and they both are sound asleep. Right on, cue the baby starts fussing, and Billy wakes up and realizes he needs to be feed. Once Doug has been fed and changed, Billy decides to keep him in his lap. Soon both are sound asleep again. A bit after midnight, the couple returns home to find Billy and the baby asleep. Jim was just about to wake them when His wife stops him. She runs off to the bedroom, gets her camera, takes some pictures, then takes the baby and puts him in bed. Then returns with a blanket and covers Billy.

The next morning, Jim takes Billy back to the airfield.

"Thanks, Billy, we had a great time," said Jim.

"Oh, it's ok, it was different watching the squirt, and it wasn't so bad."

"Don't tell my wife that or she'll be trying to get you married off to some gal."

"Not for me, thank you!" stammers Billy.

"It's about what I thought. You know my wife took a picture of you with the baby when she came home last night."

"What! She took my picture, why?"

"Who knows, but her wheels were turning, I could see it in her eyes."

"I think I'd rather go fly the canyon again."

"We're here, Billy; I have to get that fuselage done today, so I'd better get going."

"See you around Jim; I have some more work to be done on my plane before it'll be ready to fly."

Several days later, Billy has his plane finished. Billy pushes his aircraft out of the hangar to do a startup. As it just so happens that Dave and I are in the coffee shop watching Billy, as he taxi's around the tarmac and then gets permission to take off for a test hop. Then Billy lines up his plane down the runway and takes off. Billy does a roundabout flight to check out the controls and how well the Bee Gee handles. Then he lands the plane. Tomorrow Billy will retrace his flight-path to the other two cities, and come back home.

"Well, Billy, how did she handle?" asked Dave.

"Well, I'm going to put her to her paces tomorrow, and retrace my route for my check flight."

"You're not going to fly the Canyon, are you?"

"I don't plan on it."

"Good then I won't waste my time trying to talk you out of it," said Jim

"Thanks."

"How'd you like to come home to dinner with me tonight? Please!"

"Why?" asks Billy.

"Let's say you'll get a good meal, and my wife has ordered me to bring you home with me, and I want to keep her happy."

"At the expense of your friend," says Billy.

After some pleading from Jim, Billy gives in to the invitation, at least Billy knows what to expect. Billy dresses for dinner and rides in with Jim to Jim's house, they enter the house, and A young red-headed girl with Aqua colored eyes greets them at the door. Both men are brought up short, and Billy has a hard time swallowing. Doris astounds him.

"Come in, please," said Doris.

Billy almost trips over his feet upon entering, and Doris notices his awkwardness and smiles. After dinner, Jim takes Doris aside, and tells her that Billy is not interested in her, Billy has his agenda, and it involves the Sky Pirates. He doesn't want to join them; he wants to stop them.

Doris is infatuated with Billy. Doris thinks this is the first time a boy has been interested in her. Billy's modesty and honesty has stuck her as well. The picture of Billy sleeping with the baby captures her heart. She is determined to win his affection. Billy couldn't keep his eyes off Doris; she is the prettiest girl he's ever seen. He's interested, but his main focus is taking down the Sky Pirates.

The next day Doris shows up at Jim's hangar.

"Where can I find Billy?"

"Girl, you should give up and let him go," said Jim

Doris gives Jim a penetrating look.

"Ok, I guess you'll have to find out the hard way. Billy owns the last hangar in this row."

"Thank you, Mr. Collins."

Doris walks to Billy's hangar and he is just coming out of his living quarters, putting on his shirt.

"Whoa, what Are you doing here, Doris?"

"I came by to see where you worked and to visit."

"I'm sorry, Doris, but I've got a lot of work to do, and I have a trip to make in my new plane."

"Can I come with you?"

"Not really, you see that Bee Gee over there, it only holds one person. Me."

"Billy, I'm here to visit you, you can't go running off."

"Doris, you didn't tell me you were coming, and I've other plans. I'm going to do my flight check for my Bee Gee. I'll see you around."

Billy does not walk to the Bee-Gee. He almost sprints to his aircraft.

Doris is making him uncomfortable. Billy taxis out the hangar and down to the end of the tarmac, and waits until his turn comes, he takes off and flies off on his first leg of his journey. Once in the air, he manages to relax and put Doris aside in his thoughts. Billy then concentrates on flying. The first leg of his trip is uneventful, and his Bee Gee performs excellently. Upon landing in the large city, Billy decides to take a tour; he didn't want to return to his hometown, for fear that Doris would be waiting for him. Just as he was about to leave on a bus, he hears gunfire, and he looks up to see an airliner being attacked by Sky Pirates. Without any thought, Billy gets back into his Bee Gee and takes off.

Chapter

3

Billy flies up to where the Sky Pirates are, and the last plane is doing the shooting, so Billy flies above him and uses his aircraft to force the pirate down to the ground causing the pirate to crash land. Billy flies up to bring down another Pirate's plane when from behind Billy, he is being shot at by the pirates. Billy pulls in behind one of the other Pirate planes, and just as the pirate behind him starts to fire at him, Billy pulls his aircraft into a straight-up climb, and the pirate shoots down his own man. The last Sky Pirate sees his companions are gone and decides to get away. Before he leaves, the Pirate damages the airliner in hopes it'll give him time to get away. Billy looks around and sees the last Sky Pirate flying away. Billy gets ready to force the last pirate down. When Billy sees the airliner's right-wing start to dip, Billy couldn't see all those people crash and die, so Billy maneuvers his Bee Gee under the right-wing of the Air Liner and slowly using his plane he manages to help tip the wing up to a level position. The Pilot of the Air Liner brings in the aircraft for a landing, and just before it touches the ground, Billy flies out from under the wing, and the Air Liner drops to the ground. The airliner crashes, and it has much less damaged than it would've. With just a few bumps and bruises, everyone walks away from the crash.

Billy lands his damaged plane, it'll need some work done on it, his canopy is damaged, and some of his rudder was damaged, oh well at least he can fix it. When Billy lands and comes to a stop. A bunch of reporters mugs him, and some of the people from the crashed airliner. Billy was inundated with questions; he was beginning to think he liked it better being shot at by the pirates, than having to put up with all this attention. The police arrive and cart him off the field, and Billy is more than willing to go with them. Once at the station, they question Billy about the pirates, and the two he brought down were dead. They killed themselves. Billy was not able to answer many of their questions, and they let him go. One officer offered to take him back to the airfield.

Back at the airfield, a man in a suit approaches Billy.

"That was some flying you were doing, young man. You saved a hundred people from dying."

"Thank you, Sir, but right now, I don't have time for this conversation; I have to get my plane repaired."

"Well, today is your lucky day. I was one of the people you saved, I'll gladly pay for your parts and Labor for the repairs my man will be here shortly, I took the liberty of ordering the parts, and I'll have my man do the work. I'd like to talk to you about racing."

Billy is shocked, "Racing?"

"You could be the best flyer I've ever sponsored in a pylon race. I believe you'd win hands down."

Mr. Johnson leads Billy over to the restaurant to buy Billy's dinner and talk over his proposition while Billy's plane is being repaired at the nearby hangar.

Billy is puzzled over the idea of racing, so Johnson gives him a contract to look over. Billy decides to talk it over with Dave and Jim before he makes his decision. Shortly the mechanic comes in and tells Mr. Johnson that the repairs to Billy's plane are done. Billy thanks them, retires to his aircraft, and checks over the repairs made to his plane. Satisfied with the repairs, Billy gets into his plane and flies out to his next destination.

Billy encounters no other incidents in his return flight home. When he lands at the terminal, it's dark, and only the night crew is there. Billy heads to bed and sleeps until Doris rudely awakens him the next morning.

"What are you doing in my room?" exclaims Billy.

"Waking you up silly," cooed Doris

"Get out. I don't have any clothes on!"

Doris turns way and smiles, and then she leaves the room. Fifteen minutes later, Billy comes out into the hangar area. Doris leaps into his arms and plants a kiss on his cheek, then blushes and steps back.

"What was that all about?" asked Billy.

"I heard the news that you saved an airliner from crashing and that you drove off the Sky Pirates all by yourself," said Doris breathlessly.

"Doris, it's not a big deal; I only did what I had to, nothing more," said Billy exasperated.

At about that time, Jim and Dave came running into the hangar, both of them trying to catch their breath.

"We came as soon as we heard what happened, we just wanted to see if you were alright. I see Doris beat us here," said Jim.

"Guys, it's fine. The media is blowing it out of proportion. Besides, I'm glad you two are here, Mr. Johnson wants to sign a contract with me to race planes. I have the contract here in my pocket; I need to make sure there is nothing hidden in it. Will you help me?"

"Sure, Kid, you bet we will, now we best be going, we'll see you later, Billy."

Billy turns to Doris, "None of that girl, you just scoot off to home, I've work to do here, and I don't need you here in the way," said Billy sternly.

Doris looking around the hangar and seeing that it is empty, "What work? I don't see any work in here."

"It's guy stuff, now please go!"

Doris screws up her face and starts crying. (A woman's secret weapon) and runs out of the hangar.

Billy feels about two inches tall about now and almost follows her. Instead, he returns to his room to clean up from yesterday. Billy is now feeling better, except for yelling at Doris, that is.

Billy throws up his hands, "WOMEN!" and walks off towards Jim's hangar to talk over the contract.

Jim watches Doris run out of the hangar and towards her car. He watches as she fires it up and peels out of the parking lot. Then Jim sees Billy as he heads in his direction.

"Hi Jim, can you help me?"

"With what, the girl or the contract?"

"The contract, I'll wait a while before I try to tackle the girl problem."

"Probably a smart move on your part Billy. As to the contract, let's go see a lawyer, and let him look it over."

"Sounds good to me, Jim."

After the visit with the lawyer, it appears the contract is above board, so Billy contacts Mr. Johnson and agrees to fly for him. Two days later, Mr. Johnson shows up to collect the contract and to direct Billy to his hangar in the Delta city complex. Billy thinks this is a good thing. It'll get him away from Doris and let him see more of the world. Now in the background, some of the Sky Pirates are watching Billy, they cannot afford to have anyone outdo them or stop them, so this Billy Webber guy will have to die, or others may follow his example.

Billy lands at Delta city and taxis up to Johnson's hangar, where Mr. Johnson's aid greets him, she's almost as pretty as Doris is, but she ignores Billy and leads him down the hall to Mr. Johnson's Office.

Getting up from his desk, "Billy, it's good to see you made it, I'll have Cindy take you to your room and then take you on a tour of the area. Then tomorrow, we'll go over the racing schedule."

"Thank you, Mr. Johnson."

"Billy, call me Ted; after all, you did save my life."

"Anything you say, Ted."

Cindy leads Billy down to the hangar then down into a basement, where she shows him to a room where he'll be staying. Then she takes him on a tour of the whole complex, after a couple of hours of touring Cindy brings Billy back to his apartment.

"Is there anything I can get for you, Mr. Webber?"

"No Thanks, Cindy, and just call me Billy."

"Billy, you were the one who saved all those people from crashing?" Her eyes were smoldering as she pressed up close to Billy.

"Ahh. Yeah. I guess I did," and Cindy presses closer. "Cindy, you are a whole lot faster than Doris; please don't take this wrong. Please Leave."

Cindy looks into his eyes and starts laughing, and she turns and walks out of the room. Leaving Billy very red-faced and confused.

Cindy returns to Ted's office, "well, how'd it go?' asks Ted.

"He is quite the child yet, he has never been with a woman before, and he even told me to leave."

"That could prove useful in the future."

Billy turns in to get some much-needed sleep; it has been a long day; tomorrow, he has to prove he's worthy of being on the flying team.

Sky Pirates are also biding their time, so they can get even with Billy for stopping their plans of robbing that Air Liner.

Chapter

4

The next morning Billy is up and ready to fly; he has checked over his plane and waits in the ready-room to see what he has to do for flying-team and what the rules will allow. There are three kinds of races. The first one is the pylon race, where you fly around the pylons and try to be first to the finish line with all the other planes and with the best time. The second race is a long-distance run, trying to beat the clock. The third race in the canyon run, and if you survive and have the best time, you win. All of the heats are dangerous; People get killed in these races. Billy isn't concerned about the other fliers out flying him.

Back in his office, Ted is talking to his board of representatives or stockholders.

"Who's this Billy Webber we keep hearing about?" Asked the board.

"He is the pilot who saved the Air Liner I was on; he also downed two of three Sky Pirates."

"You realize Ted that they'll try to kill him in revenge for what he did."

"I know, and I'm counting on it. It'll spice up the race, and bring more people to watch, especially if they believe they can see someone die."

"Does this new pilot Billy Webber know of this death threat?"

"No, and I'm not going to tell him either."

"Your scheme may work, the media has dubbed this boy a flying wonder that alone will make people interested in coming to the race to see the man who drove off the Sky Pirates, and saved the Air Liner."

"We need to keep this quiet and from Billy, or he may choose not to fly. Today he's in the Ready Room waiting for instructions; I'm going to have him fly the canyon for practice."

"Ok, Ted, we'll leave it in your hands."

Billy wasn't much on carrying a weapon, but he knew that the Sky Pirates would be looking to kill him because of what he did; he's looking for a way to draw them out into the open. Billy wants to know more about them and is hoping to bring one down alive so he can question him. Back at the Landing field where he saved the Air Liner, Billy manages to get to collect one of the Pirates blasters just as the pirate kills himself. Billy had then removed the pirate's blaster and holster. When the police came up to capture the pirate, Billy tells them the pirate had killed himself. Billy walked off with the blaster and holster. At first, the Policeman was going to stop Billy but changed his mind. Billy will need it to protect himself figures the police officer and says nothing.

Billy decides to go to the police station, and Billy tells them who he is and that he'd like to learn how to use the weapon he captured. Is there someone here who'd train him so he'd not hurt himself or others when he used it? A passing police officer hears him and then asks him why, and Billy relates why he wants to learn how to use the blaster.

"Son, I'll help you. That Air Liner you saved was carrying my wife and kid, and except for a few bruises, they're just fine. For that alone, I'll help you."

The officer takes Billy into the basement and walks through the basics of the weapon, holding it and firing it. "Now one thing you need to know Billy; accuracy counts more than speed. Get the accuracy down the speed will follow. Now one thing else, practice what I've shown you, and if you're in a dogfight, make sure to lead your target. Now let me show you how to break down your weapon and put it back together. Billy should also practice this, so you can do this in the dark, especially if it jams."

Billy leaves to practice what the officer told him to practice. At the compound, Billy finds an out of the way place to practice his accuracy. After weeks of training, he could hit his target wherever he wanted, and he could disassemble and reassemble his gun in the dark with his eyes closed. In between times, Billy practiced his flying; he would fly over to the canyon and fly through it from one end to another, practicing low-level flying. What Billy didn't know is that the race manager is building Billy up as a great hero, and the one who drove off the Sky Pirates. The manager wants publicity for his race, and what better way to advertise it so the Sky

Pirates will show up and try to kill Billy. The next race is in a few days; it would be the pylon race. Also watching are the Secret Police; they want the Sky Pirates badly, so Billy is to be the bait, thanks to Ted Johnson.

The day of the race comes, and Billy is in last place, seeing as he is a new flyer. The ten planes lined up on the runway waiting for permission to take off; once in the air, the aircraft will fly in formation until everyone is off the ground. Then the checkered flag will drop, and the race will begin. The point to this race is to beat the clock and each other. They'll fly around the three pylons trying to pass each other without crashing into one another. The laps are usually ten times around the pylons and the winners who makes it will be the ones with the best time and position to win the race. The flag drops, and off they go. Right off the two planes just in front of Billy fly into each other and down they go. Now they're down to eight aircraft. After flying for a few minutes, Billy decides to climb somewhat higher. Billy knows the laser cameras will track him to see if he flies outside the parameters of the race, and he manages to pass overhead and gets by four more of the racers; by the fifth lap, Billy has caught up to the leaders, and he drops down behind them. By the seventh lap, Billy passes the second lead plane and is right behind the first leader. With three laps to go, Billy sits back for the next two laps, and on the last lap, Billy guns his airplane by diving close to the ground, and the power-dive gives Billy just enough speed to pass the leader. Then make it to the finish line, and it's a photo finish, with Billy winning the race by a whisker.

The Sky Pirates don't show, at least they didn't try to kill Billy during the race. They were there watching, and they saw the Secret Police there as well. All the Sky Pirates want at this time; is to observe and see how good this Billy is. The Secret Police are in the stands scanning the crowd to see if they can spot the Pirates. One of the pirates walks by the secret police and doesn't draw any attention to themselves. One pirate, however, bumps into a police officer and apologizes, he even stops for a moment to talk to the police officer about the race. Then moves on just like anyone else. By this time, Billy is at the winner's circle receiving his trophy and the purse. The next race is to be the long-distance race, where you have to beat the clock.

5

"Well, Kids, do you mind if I take a moment to wet my whistle with this ice-cold Cider."

Grandfather takes a long pull on the cider he is drinking and then wipes his mouth with the back of his hand. "That's more like it, now where were we. Oh yes, the next race is the long-distance race where you have to beat the clock to the three destinations." Billy is the first one in line since he had just won the pylon race. The first leg of the race goes very well; Billy is ahead only by a few seconds. The next leg Billy's plane has been tampered with, his crystal has been misaligned, and so it'll not turn over the engine properly.

"Now, as I recall, Billy lost his place in the lineup, and some points were deducted from him." Billy sets out to find out why his engine is having problems and soon discovers his problem, so he aligns the crystal as well as he can by eye, which he did most of the time anyway. Billy is shifted to the back of the line. When his time comes up, he takes off and flies right off to the next destination. To save time, Billy climbs high into the air, where it is frigid, and the atmosphere is thin. He flies most of the race that way. Then Billy dives straight down on to the airfield using as much speed as he can. Billy manages to come up with the fastest time; he can move back into first place with an even more significant gap in time over the leader. That night Billy decides to sleep with his plane; no one is going to tamper with his plane again. It's all quiet in the hangar where Billy is sleeping. Then he hears a door open; Billy moves away from his plane and into the shadows to watch. Sure, enough, the two pilots who're just behind him are sneaking up on his plane. Billy pulls out his blaster, and when one of them opens an access panel on his aircraft. Billy speaks up.

"Gentlemen, how kind of you to inspect my plane, now stop what you're doing and turn around. I see the leaders in the race. What should I do, accuse you to the commission, or let you go?"

"Yes, let us go." They both plead.

"I guess I will, but be mindful, if anything happens to my plane, you'll take the full brunt of my anger."

Billy Takes aims at the tool the men were going to use on his plane, and he fires the blaster turning the tool into molten metal.

"Now gentlemen consider what might happen if I shot your plane or you for that matter. Now get out of here."

The two leave quickly. The next morning the two men did everything they could to stay away from Billy.

The launch of the final leg of the race happens early the next morning, an hour before the race begins Billy is approached by two other men (They're the secret police) We would like to talk with you in private, and they showed Billy their badges.

Billy looks at them for a few minutes then said, "Sure; why not. What can I do for you?"

"We have information that the Sky Pirates are going to attack the racers near the canyon."

"Oh, and you don't want me to fly?"

"No, we want you to fly; you're our bait to bring them out of hiding."

"What'll you do when they come out?"

"We hope you'll survive; we'd like you to join our ranks if you manage to live through this race."

"I'll keep that in mind when I win this race."

"Please do, we're serious we're hoping to convince you to fake your death so that we can use you as a spy for us against the pirates."

"I'll give it some thought," mused Billy.

Billy leaves them to go, Billy make sure his plane is ready to fly, and to make sure nothing else is on board like a bomb. After going through the aircraft from one end to the other, he does not find any explosives, tracking devices, or the like. His plane is clean; what Billy didn't know is that a tracker was placed on him, not his plane. Sometime during the night. Someone had borrowed his jacket and placed the homer in a tear along a seam of his coat.

When the time comes to start the race, Billy is first to takeoff. After he clears the end of the runway, the next plane will follow, and so on. At the end of the runway, a small group of men will write down the time they left for the time calculations at the end of the race. Billy is in the lead and knows he's being followed. Off his right-wing is an aircraft, and one-off his left-wing, they're at a distance, but they're still there. Billy figures that they're Sky Pirates, and they're going to start making their move when Billy gets over the canyon. Billy decides that he'll leave the race to keep others from being endangered. Billy changes his heading towards the canyon, and heads for the eye of the needle, Billy threaded it once, why not again. Billy catches them off guard as he dives toward the ground, so he gains some speed and manages to get ahead of them.

Now, this is a race for his life. A blaster from one of the men sizzled past his cockpit, so Billy takes evasive action to avoid other shots. Billy thought of returning fire, but he needs to concentrate on his flying, he'd soon be at the canyon. Billy arrives at the canyon and pulls his aircraft into a power climb, which catches the Pirates by surprise, and they try to follow him. At two thousand feet, Billy does a hammerhead and goes into a dive for the ground; he did this to gain some more speed, and hopefully, surprise. Billy heads for the canyon at the point of entry Billy has to have his wings vertical to the ground as he enters the canyon. The first Pirate's plane tries to follow Billy on his tail, manages to hit the edge of the canyon, and crashed into a wall. The other Pirate flies above the canyon still following Billy, and from time to time, the Pirate would take a shot at Billy in hopes of hitting him. Now Billy has less wind resistance and is picking up some distance on the Pirate, the pirate watches, and he notices that the eye of the needle will soon be coming up and that

Billy will crash against the wall of the canyon.

The Pirate keeps shooting at Billy to keep him in the canyon. Billy sees the eye, dives right into it, inverts his wings again, and Billy threads the needle. After Billy passes through, he pulls back on the stick and does a power climb straight up, catching the Pirate by surprise, causing him to take evasive action to avoid hitting the mountain. Billy turns his plane upside down, passing over the Pirate and shoots the Pirate's engine sending him into a crash. Billy comes around, lands his plane, and runs to the Pirate. Billy wants some answers. The Pirate crawls out of his aircraft and realizes he is severely injured. Then the Pirate spots Billy coming towards him, and he fires at Billy with his blaster, Billy ducks, and fires back. The Pirate realizes he's about to be captured, and puts the blaster to his head and pulls the trigger. When Billy arrives, the Pirate is dead. Then Billy decides to take the secret police upon their proposition for him to die and join their service. Billy removes his clothes, and his identification then puts them on the Pirate and puts the clothes of the dead Pirate on, and Billy takes the Pirate's blaster.

Chapter

6

Billy drags the dead Pirate back to the Pirate's plane and fires at it a few more times to make it look like it had been shot down in the battle. Then Billy gets back into his plane and flies off toward the secret police's headquarters. The next day, Billy's death is in all the newspapers. "Here now, let me take another pull at that cider. Now where was I, oh yeah?" says Grandfather.

Billy's death hits Doris hard, she had hopes of marrying Billy, and it was just not to be. She moved on after a few years, and she had a few children by a doctor who she had married. Well anyway, Billy turns up at the secret police headquarters, where they take great pains to hide his Identity. Then the secret police put Billy through a lot of training most of its physical training, and some of it is just learning how to fight. Billy is taught to use all the gadgets they're going to give him. Billy realizes all this training is to give him a chance to survive his up and coming mission. When they're done with him each day he can barely walk; he's so tired from the workouts he's ready to drop off to sleep, the secret police encouraged Billy to grow a beard to cover his face, and then they loaded him up with all kinds of gadgets. They replaced his plane with a newly captured Pirate aircraft, and they have the science group add to it. Billy's mission is to discover who the leader is and where they're hold up. If possible, to capture this mysterious leader and bring them in for justice.

As the mission begins, Billy is instructed to go to a particular bar on the outskirts of an airfield where rumor has it that he might find a Sky Pirate. Billy enters and orders a whiskey and sits alone in a dark corner of the smoky room so he can watch the people in the bar. Billy dressed in a flight jacket and old one at that, a pair of worn-out trooper pants, and an old pair of flight boots. Billy puts his feet up on the table and slowly drinks his whiskey; a plain-looking girl approaches him and asks if he wants anything else. He tells her that he wants to be left alone, so she goes away. Then a man approaches to offer him another drink. "What is it with you people, I wish to be left alone," and Billy stands up and shoves the guy away. Of course, this starts a fight, and it seems everyone wants to be involved. A short time later, the police arrive to put a stop to the fighting. Billy takes a police stick across his face breaking his nose. Billy and the others who were fighting are taken to jail. While Billy is in the medical wing of the police station being patched up, he's called to the courtroom for sentencing. He's placed in front of the judge, and just as the sentencing is just about to be passed, there's a commotion in the back of the room, and a lawyer approaches the bench. After a few whispered words, the lawyer leads Billy out of the courtroom.

"Hey what gives?" said Billy

"A friend has paid your bail and would like to talk to you."

"Where?" asks Billy.

"I'll take you."

"I guess; let's go, the police make me itch."

They leave the station, and the lawyer drives him to an expensive hotel across town and ushers Billy up to the top floor and into a suite. Billy is asked to sit down, and he does, Billy appears relaxed, but he wasn't. Billy is concerned for his life and is as tight as a spring wound up and ready to spring loose. The lawyer hands Billy another whiskey and leaves the room. Soon one of the men from the bar steps in from the far end of the room.

"I see you took a slight beating from the police, are you alright?"

"I'm just fine; why'd you spring me from jail?" asks Billy.

"You might say I'm a recruiter for an employer, and you seem to fit the need we have."

"What need is that?"

"After some checking, we'll let you know. For now, you stay here and enjoy yourself. If you pass inspection, so to speak, you'll find out all you need to know at that time."

"What if I don't pass inspection?"

"No need to talk about unpleasant things just yet. Now is there anything you'd like before I leave?"

"Not at all," answered Billy.

"Good, I'll return in a few days if you think of anything you want. The man outside your door will get it."

"Ok, I will."

"Oh, before I forget, don't leave this room, the man outside will shoot to kill, those are his orders."

"Thanks for telling me, I'd sure hate to have a misunderstanding," said Billy.

Billy was stuck cooling his heels in the hotel room, waiting to see if he'd be accepted or killed, which came with the job. As Billy is musing, a red-light appears on the wall behind him; he gets a closer look. In the center of the dot is a code word. Billy turns to the window and waves. The red-light goes out then comes back with a different message. Are you in?" nod for yes, and shake your head back and forth for no. Billy did not have an answer for them, so he shrugged. It seems they got the message; the red-light goes out.

Not long after, the man outside the door opened it to check on Billy, and Billy is just getting another whiskey.

"Is everything alright, sir?"

"You don't have to call me, sir; Ace will do."

"Whatever you say, Ace."

"I'm doing fine, thank you for asking," replies Ace.

The guard closes the door and locks it. Ace looks around the room and spots a radio, so he turns it on to listen to some music. The next morning, Billy is getting antsy. Every noise gives him a start. Finally, the lawyer shows up at the door.

"Your Ace Williams, you have quite a rap sheet I see robbery, murder suspect, and other things. I have a glowing report on you. You're just the kind of person my employer is looking for."

"So, who do I have to kill to get in?" questions Billy.

"For right now, no one. You'll be leaving here today, and in a few days, you'll meet our boss."

"It's kind of strange to get recruited for a job, and I haven't met the client," states Billy.

"If I were you, I wouldn't get too nosy; it can be fatal if you know what I mean."

"I understand," says Billy.

"Good! Now get some sleep, tomorrow will be a long day."

"Yes, Sir." Ace salutes the lawyer, with a sarcastic smirk on his face.

One thing is for sure the next day was a long day; they got Billy (Ace) up before dawn and is asked if he had a plane; he can fly.

"Yes, and it's ready to go."

"Good!" said the guard, "which airfield is it?"

"It's at the local airfield, the international one has too many police watching and looking for me," says Ace.

"There's a car outside the building in the alley, get there and catch your ride, someone will be at the airfield to give you further orders."

Ace finishes getting dressed and leaves to meet the car. Ace gets into the car and drives off to the airfield, only to arrive an hour later.

"You sure took a long way around, is someone following us?" asked Ace.

The driver says nothing. Ace shrugs and walks over to his plane. Then Ace sees a mechanic checking his plane over.

"Hey, what are you doing? No one touches my plane except me."

The mechanic turns to face Ace, and Ace realizes it's one of the instructors from the secret police school.

"I've checked everything, sir, and it's all in working order."

Ace flips a coin to the mechanic. "Ok, in the future, don't touch my plane."

"Yes, sir."

Just then, two men approach Billy (Ace).

"What is going on?"

"A mechanic is trying to make some money off me by checking my plane over for me."

Ace starts to preflight his plane, and the two men followed him as he does, they are checking for bugs or electronic beacons that may have been placed on the plane.

"Hey, what's this?" Ace pulls a strange looking item from a compartment and shows it to the men.

"That's a tracker; we'll check the rest of your plane," said one of the men.

They opened all the access panels and compartments checking for other tracking devices, they found nothing. What they didn't know is that Ace has a tracker in his coats lining.

"Well, Ace, we're giving you a clean Billy of health, now we are going to add our device, it's a bomb. If for any reason, you deviate from our formation today, we'll blow you right out of the sky."

"Ok, I got it; you don't trust me or my reputation," said Ace.

"No, we don't trust you. Neither does the boss, so if you want to meet him, do it our way."

"Fair enough, when do we leave, and where are we going

next?" questions Ace.

"You'll taxi to the end of the runway and wait, in a few moments a plane like yours will taxi onto the field, and take off. Follow him to the destination. If you deviate from following, he'll either shoot you down or blow up your plane."

"I get the picture," stated Ace.

Ace does what he's told; he waits at the end of the runway and soon another plane much like his own taxis up and readies to take off. After clearing with the tower, the aircraft runs down the runway and leaps into the air, followed shortly by Ace. As they fly along, Ace removes the tracking device from his coat and places it under his seat.

Chapter

7

"Well, kids, I need to stand up and walk around a bit, freshen up," says grandpa.

Grandpa takes a drink of cider and then walks into the house to the bathroom, and as he comes out, Jeff is standing outside the door.

"Grandpa, if Billy (Ace) was thought dead, how is it you know about this part of the story?"

"Sharp Kid, aren't you. Well, you'll have to wait until further into the story."

"Awa Grandpa, can't you tell me now?"

"No, Jeff, you'll have to wait," said grandpa.

They walk back to the table outside and sit down; grandpa takes another drink to get his thoughts collected before he launches back into the story.

"Ok, Billy or Ace, if you will; was following the Pirate's plane to the next destination."

They fly the next day to the edge of our continent. Land at an out of the way landing strip.

Ace gets out of his plane and checks it over, doing a post-flight check to make sure the aircraft is ready to fly the next day. Ace is directed to a bunkhouse to sleep off the flight, and in a few hours, they'll wake him up for some food. Before Ace goes back to sleep, Ace explores the area, noting the buildings, and the people he sees. The Secret Police know of this place, and so Ace doesn't bother to leave a tracer here. Ace walks around outside for some fresh air when he sees someone on his plane. Ace walks over and asks, "what's going on?"

"What're you doing to my plane?" asks Ace.

"Basic Maintenance and sweeping for bugs."

"Bugs?"

"Yes, the Secret Police always manages to plant bugs on some of these planes, or the person flying the plane may be a spy. We had one once, and he almost got away with it."

"Continue, your scan; I sure don't want to have a bug on my plane. The Secret Police has too much on me as it is. They'd lock me up and throw away the key if they caught me. Here maybe you should scan me to make sure I've not been bugged."

The Mechanic scans Ace and finds nothing. "You're clean."

"Oh, good, may I get in my plane. I left my gun under the seat, and I'd feel better carrying it," said Ace.

"Sure, go ahead."

Ace reaches under his seat, pulls out his gun and the tracking device, and returns to the bunkhouse. At dawn, everyone is awakened and told to get dressed and report to the mess hall for breakfast. It'll be a long flight with no stops until we get to our final destination, so they were all told to eat well. Within the hour, they'd be leaving, on their last leg of the flight, so they should preflight their planes. Like the other pilots, Ace does a preflight on his aircraft, noting that guns have been added and some jamming gear. When Ace has finished, he stands by his plane like the other pilots, waiting for the instruction to mount and fire up the aircraft. The orders are given, and the ten pilots board their aircraft and start them up. The leader boards his plane and is ready to taxi out on to the runway, followed by other pilots. One by one, each plane lifts off and meets up with the leader. Once everyone is in the air.

"Leader to all pilots. You may not return to the airfield; if you do, you'll be shot down. Also, some of you'll not make it to the final destination. Some of you'll crash into the ocean. This last leg is to see who can make it, an endurance flight if you like. If you make it, you'll be received as a Sky Pirate, or you'll die. No further talking and follow me if you can."

"Man, that is thirsty work, doing all that talking. Are you getting all this story down son, I'd hate to have to do a full repeat of this story?"

"I'm getting it all pop."

Grandpa takes another swallow of the cold cider, wipes his mouth off with the back of his hand, and scratches at his chin in thought.

"Now, where was I?"

"You're going to tells us about the long flight."

"Oh, yes, that's right."

Billy is at the tail end of the flight squadron, winging its way to its unknown destination except for the leader. They left the land behind and flew out over open water. Soon there were no landmarks to steer by. (*Now the planes on this world don't use fuel to fly, it gets its energy from crystals and capacitors which store the energy the crystals get from the sun. The capacitors can hold enough power until the sun comes up in the morning. As long as you do not use the planes blaster, this'll put a drain on the energy.*)

Ace has a suspicion that they'll be attacked, to see what the pilots will do. Ace breaks formation and flies above the rest of the squadron.

"This is the leader speaking; cadet get back in formation!"

"Sir Bogeys at the starboard side, Two-O-clock low. What're your orders?"

"Scatter, and take out the bogeys."

Ace from on high comes down and takes out the lead plane, then pulls up and takes out the last plane. As calculated, some of the other pilots from the Sky Pirates squadron are shot down. Most of the bogeys are either shot down or driven off. Ace having done the lion's share of the shooting.

"Well, cadet, that's some mighty fine shooting, too bad though, you'll not have enough power to make it to the last destination."

"Lead on, sir, I'll follow. I may surprise you," said Ace.

You see kids Billy while he was walking around the hidden airport, found another plane that was being worked on and pulled the planes capacitor and charged it just in case; he'd need it.

Chapter

8

The planes that're left of the squadron. Are flying along when one plane stops working and drops from the sky into the ocean below. Ace then decides to plug in his extra capacitor to keep from doing the same thing. Now the other problem is that the pilots are getting tired. Another one falls asleep and crashes into the ocean as well, leaving the leader and three planes. Hours go by and still no land in sight, when the leader pulls his airplane into a steep climb, followed by the remaining flyers. From out of the clouds, a Zeppelin appears, and the leader flies up to the top of the Zeppelin and lands on the wooden deck. Once the other three pilots see what the leader has done, they also follow his lead and land on the top deck.

"This is why the secret police cannot find the base; it's on a Zeppelin." Thinks Ace.

On the Zeppelin, Ace and the other two pilots are hustled to the Zeppelin's interior, and soon to another barracks within the ship. Hot food is sent to them, and they're allowed to sleep. Ace is grateful for that; he's dog tired; this is the first time he has had to fly that long a distance without sleep. Ten hours later, Ace and the two other pilots are summoned to the Ready Room (a room onboard ship where orders and assignments are given).

"Sit down cadets; you made the cut. You survived to make it here to the Zeppelin. You've demonstrated that you have what it takes to be a sky pirate. Your training will continue tomorrow, and it'll be extensive. You three have the rest of the day to settle in. Sargent takes these men and get them back to their assignments."

"Yes, sir."

The Sargent forms up the men and marches them out of the Ready Room, and takes them to supply to get their uniforms and equipment. Once they have all their gear, they are marched to another barracks where they are assigned a bunk. Then they're taken on a tour of the ship to all the training rooms. Then back to the barracks. Where they spend the rest of the day getting settled in place, like anywhere, the people who want to be in charge, try to bully the new people. This place is no exception, so the biggest guy shakes down the recruits to get them into the pecking order at the bottom. Ace being small in build figures that he'll be the target for this bully. He's not wrong. The big man grabs Ace by the front of his shirt and hauls him out of bed. Ace is trying to keep his temper under control, but this buffoon is making it complicated. (the secret police gave Ace specialized training on how to fight) Ace latches onto the big guys' wrist and, with the proper amount of force, pinches a nerve causing the guy to open his hand.

"Now, are we done playing this game? If you want to be the big guy in charge, good, just leave me alone, and we'll get along just fine," stated Ace.

The big guy gets mad and tries to plant a haymaker to Ace's stomach. Ace sidesteps and applies a Big extra force and sends the big guy into a wall headfirst, which knocks him out cold.

Ace whence, "That must've hurt."

Ace gets back on his bunk and starts to read a book. In a short time, the big guy gets up and is mad. He starts to walk over to Ace's bunk, when Ace holds up a finger and says, "If I were you, I'd stop right there and walk away."

Ace looks up into the big guy's eyes, stopping him in his tracks. The big guy starts laughing and holds out his hand to Ace, and Ace takes it.

"Could you teach me how to do that?" asks the big guy.

"If you want to learn I can, my name is Ace, what's yours?"

Pointing both thumbs at his chest, "They call me Bruiser."

"Good name that. It's been a long trip getting here, and I could use some rest."

So, Bruiser walks back to his bunk and stares everybody into being quiet, Ace closes his eyes and goes over in his mind what he has to do, to get to the top man. Ace drops off to sleep; a few hours later, Bruiser shakes Ace awake.

"Chow time Ace and we need to get into line."

"Thank you, Bruiser."

The line is rather long, and the food smells good, so they wait in line to get their food.

"Would you like to take cuts, Ace?"

"No, Bruiser, consider this a start in your training."

"How is that, Ace?"

"It's called patients, it's the toughest thing to learn, but it'll be worth it in the long run. We'll wait until it's our turn."

"Ok, Ace, we'll do it your way."

They get their food and soon occupy a place someone just vacated, and Ace with Bruiser sits down to eat.

"Well, Bruiser, what can you tell me about being a Sky Pirate."

"It's like being in the military Ace, they teach us to fly, fight, and rob from the rich and keep it to ourselves."

"Who runs the Sky Pirates?"

"The Queen, she controls the whole operation."

"A woman?"

"Yes, a woman. She is tough and ruthless. I watched her take down a man as big as me with her bare hands, and then kill him."

"Just like that?" asks Ace.

"Yea, just like that." Bruiser snaps his fingers.

"I'd like to meet our Queen."

"Just be glad that you don't, the only people who meet the Queen are people who distinguish themselves and become trusted people she keeps or people who fail and are killed by her to prove her power."

"I can distinguish myself," said Ace.

"Don't do that, Ace. In most cases, it becomes a death sentence. Because she always wants your loyalty to be absolute. When she tires of one of these people, she has them do suicide missions."

"Thanks for the warning Bruiser, I'll keep that in mind."

They finish their meal, and Ace asks Bruiser to take them to a training area to teach Bruiser how to fight using the secret police fighting style.

Bruiser asks Ace how he learned this type of fighting.

Thinking fast, Ace told Bruiser about being in the paramilitary and had to learn to fight like that because most of the missions were without weapons, except for a knife.

"Why're you not still in the military?" asks Bruiser.

"I was on a mission, and I killed the wrong person, so I was drummed out of the service in disGlory."

"I see, so you can kill with this type of fighting?" asks Bruiser.

"Yes, Bruiser, we can kill using this type of fighting. Now we'll begin with exercise."

Ace is drawing on the training he received at the Secret Police headquarters to teach Bruiser.

Bruiser takes to the training quickly. Soon he learns how to use the pressure points and balance, and lastly, how to use the opponent's strength against him.

"Is this how you managed to beat me?"

"I'm afraid so Bruiser, I used you against you."

"I'm never going to throw another haymaker again."

"Then you learned what you needed to learn Bruiser, if you follow what I taught you, you'll never lose at hand to hand combat again."

"Thank you, Ace, now, we need to bring the rest of the cadets down here and train them to do this."

Ace is about to reject the idea when he sees the Captain

of the Zeppelin watching them, and Ace agrees to teach the other cadets.

The next day Ace is drug down to the training area by Bruiser, and he finds the whole group from the barracks there; some of them were not too happy to be there.

"Ace, we're here to learn your fighting skills, and Bruiser turns toward the men and says, aren't we men?"

In unison, they all agree. Ace has them form up to get ready to do the exercises as Ace walks the line of men, he sees some of the men had been persuaded vigorously, Ace almost cracks a smile, but decides not to. Over the next several weeks, Ace and Bruiser snap these Cadets into a team, which the Captain finds exceptional and disturbing.

Captain Rogers decides to test these new cadets before they even reach the island of training. The Captain calls Ace up to his bridge and tells him he'd like Ace to fight the Fleet Champion to prove how good he can fight. Ace agrees, so the fight is set to happen in a few days. Bruiser is taking bets that Ace will win the match. In the Captain's office, the Fleet Champion shows up.

"The Captain wishes to see me," said the champ.

"Yes, I want you to win this fight, and during the process of the fight, I want you to kill this upstart. Do you understand?" demands the Captain.

"Yes, sir. I'll do as you have said!"

"Good, or it'll be you who has the unfortunate accident! Dismissed."

The champion salutes the Captain and leaves his office. The Captain reaches over to the com and calls up the exec.

"Rivers, get Sabastian and come to my office," snaps the Captain.

The two men present themselves to the Captain.

"I've instructed the champion to kill this Ace person. He's becoming too popular with the men. This might under mind our plans to oust the Queen and take over the Sky Pirates. We need the men to be fearful of us so they'll obey us without question."

"Why don't we kill him outright?" asks the exec.

"We have to be careful; Ace has to die accidentally, otherwise it might call us into question before the Queen. We've worn out the excuse of everyone we kill of being a possible spy. As it is, we've killed too many that way without proof. Besides, his men might revolt, and others may follow. No Ace has to die, and it has to be an accident or at least appear to be one."

"We'll keep our eyes open for a chance then," said Sabastian.

"Ace may no longer be a problem after the fight in two days," said Captain Rogers.

During the two days, Ace trains with his men; Bruiser has placed bets wherever he can and with whoever will be willing to bet.

Bruiser comes up to Ace.

"Ace you have to win this fight, I bet so heavily that if you lose, I may be learning how to fly without a plane."

"What did you do, Bruiser?" demands Ace.

"Well, you see, I bet more money than I have, and if I lose, I cannot pay it back."

"I don't intend to lose Bruiser; I also don't want to win too fast, either." muses Ace.

On the day of the fight, Ace sees the Captain, the exec., and a strange man who is introduced as Sabastian, one of the Queen's men. Ace shakes their hands. Ace gets a bad feeling from them.

"Something is wrong here!" thinks Ace.

Chapter

9

Ace enters the ring first, as the rookie and he sees where the Captain, Exec. And Sabastian are sitting. Not too far from his water bottle. Ace watches as the champion enters the ring. Right away, Ace determines that this man is going to try to kill him, and Ace realizes it's an order from the Captain.

"I wonder what game is being played here," thinks Ace.

The bell rings, and the men square off and start sparing with each other. Ace allows the champion to get in several good licks, leaving Ace with a few cuts to the face, and some bruised ribs. Ace decides to make the fight in his favor. Using his skills as the overconfident champion attacks him, Ace puts him down on the canvas with the champion trying to catch his breath from Ace's counter punch. Ace backs off to let the champion up. The champion loses his cool and becomes enraged. No one has ever knocked him down before. The champion charges Ace, and Ace uses the champions momentum against him and sends him into one of the corner posts face-first breaking his nose. After a moment, the champion gets up, sees the blood, then becomes enraged and charges Ace like a bull. Ace sends the champion into his corner, missing the post; the champion flies through the ropes and on to the floor, breaking his neck. This ends the fight. The three men look up at Ace, realizing they've just tipped their hand.

Ace watches them leave, and the men in the audience cheer him on, all that is, but the ones who lost their bets. Two days later, the Zeppelin lands on an island, which is a type of boot camp. Where the men will have extensive training to fight, fly, and rob people. The Sky Pirates have been using this remote Island for decades. Only a few people under the Queen even know of this Island. It's so distant on this world. Ace and his cadets get to stay together as a company. They'll be trained together. As to the team leader, Ace is chosen easily. Everyone in the company elects Ace as their leader. Ace doesn't want to be their leader; he doesn't want to call attention to himself per the direction of the secret police. Now Ace realizes this may be the best way to come to the attention of the Queen. During training, Ace's company starts collecting all the honors as the best of all the companies. The Commander of the Island decides to have a war game of sorts in hopes of finding a way to discredit Ace and his team.

Captain Rogers decides to pit Ace's Company against the other three companies in the camp; the winners will get a steak for dinner for a week. Ace goes to the briefing to see what the rules are. The object of the game is to steal the Island trophy out of its case. Then get away without being caught. The game will start in the wee hours of the morning; here is a map of the Island and the building where you'll find the trophy. Ace heads back to the barracks and forms up the men and marches them out to the grinder (marching field) to talk to them.

"Hey Ace, why are we out here, and not in the barracks doing this."

"Did you see the other day some strange people in our barracks, claiming to be making repairs." queries Ace.

"Now that you mention it, yes," said a squad leader.

"They weren't repairing anything; they were putting in bugs and cameras to watch us. Probably for this very game."

"That's not right," one of the others said.

"Be that as it may, we may use it against them. We have about another hour before we'll be in the game. Some of you scatter and listen to what the other companies are saying. If they can spy on us, that means we can spy on them. We'll meet at the South end of the island in an hour, now scoot. Bruiser and Buckman come with me, we're going to play a game of our own."

Back at the barracks, Ace tells the two men in detail how they'll approach the building from the South. The men look at Ace strangely; Ace holds up his finger to quite them. Now agree with me. And they do. Ace hands a note to Buckman. Buckman reads it.

"Ace, you're telling us your plan here, won't they know what we are doing?'

Bruiser balls up his fist to hit Buckman when Ace stops him and holds up his thumb to sign that it's OK.

"Ace, what're you doing? Now they know we're coming from the South of the Island."

"Yes, Bruiser, and with your slip, they'll assume we're coming from the North. You played your part very well."

"I didn't say anything."

"No, you didn't, but they caught your reaction with Buckman, that'll throw them off. They'll concentrate their numbers in the North, and just have a few in the South, it won't be easy, but we can put enough of their men out of action so we can reach the trophy."

"We told the truth, and they'll think we lied to them?"

" Yes, rather sneaky, isn't it?" smiled Ace.

Ace meets the rest of his company at the South end of the Island at the time appointed.

"Now, men remember your training. Put everyone you come across to sleep and move toward the trophy room. The closer we get, the harder it'll be, so no talking, use the hand signals I taught you. Now let's win this so-called game." commands Ace.

They encounter few men as they move toward the buildings, using the ground cover to the best advantage they move into position. The men they meet are left tied up and gaged; some will be out for some time. One of Ace's men picked up a giant crab and is carrying it with him. One of his team looks at him questionably; he signals you'll see. They move along toward the building. They all approach the buildings and start to encounter more and more men that are looking for them. The men approached the South side of the buildings. The man with the crab pitches it across the alley, where it makes a lot of noise attracting the guards. Because of its thrashing around, and all the chittering it's making. The guards approach the sound with guns drawn to investigate. When they pass the men that were in hiding, Ace's men pounce on them and, in a few minutes, have them down and out. They strip the radios and the armbands from the fallen men. Then the man who used the crab makes a frantic call on the radio saying Ace's company coming from the North West is overwhelming them and cuts off the communication.

They lay low and wait, soon a squad of men can be seen rushing by and leave the area heading North West. After they leave, the two men walk out into the alley and head towards the trophy building, still silent when an officer brings them short.

"Attention! They stop and pop to attention. The officer approaches them and asks why they're here and not with the rest of the group headed North West.

The man who had the crab says.

"We're ordered back to guard the alley in case of a sneak attack."

"Who was it cadet that gave that order?"

"Sgt. Bennet, sir."

"I see cadet, carry on."

"Yes, sir!" and they both salute him as he walks off.

When the officer leaves, the two men continued their guarding, and soon others of their company showed up, guiding them in the direction of the trophy building.

A few minutes later, Ace and his cadets enter the building

and soon have it under their control, and they capture the trophy and a couple of officers to boot.

Ace has his men retreat, taking the trophy and the officers they've captured, and return to the South end of the Island. The next morning Ace and his company march back to headquarters with the trophy and the officers in tow. Ace presents the trophy to the Commandant, along with his two missing officers. Ace is aware that the Commandant is very upset with him for winning the war game. The Commandant takes the trophy and awards the prize to Ace's company and the steak dinners.

As it stands, Ace's company is the highest rated company of all time. The next task in training is to capture a Zeppelin in flight. The Commandant issues drawings of the Zeppelin so the company leaders can figure out a way to take the ship using the airfield airplanes. Ace takes Bruiser with him, and instead of going to the barracks, Ace takes them to the airfield to inspect the planes assigned to his company. Ace inspects all the aircraft. Then he heads back to the barracks.

"I know that look Ace, what did you figure out?" asks Bruiser.

"I'll tell you when we gather the men and go for a picnic."

"A picnic?"

"Yes, Bruiser, a picnic."

10

Confused but willing to follow Ace even into the pits of hell, Bruiser does what he's told. Ace details a couple of men to get box lunches for a hike. Soon his company is off to the South end of the island. After they arrive, Ace has the men gather around him.

"We're going to make the best time ever in taking over a Zeppelin, but I'll need your help and cooperation. Who of you are good mechanics, a couple of the men raise their hands? Good, you three go over there. Now I need a few good electricians. Very good, you go over to where the mechanics are. The rest of you eat your lunch. I'll get back to you shortly."

Ace outlines what he has in mind to the mechanics and the electricians so they can ponder the request, and soon come up with a few solutions. Ace considers and selects the one he thinks will work the best and be the safest to use. Now Ace returns to the group, and as they eat, Ace outlines what he's planning to do. Ace cautions the men not to say a word about this plan to anyone and don't discuss it in the barracks. Remember, it's bugged; we'll meet here every day as necessary. Now all the best pilots line up over here. A bit over half the company.

"Tomorrow we'll meet at the hangar, I need only half of the men to be fliers the other half will be the air marines, and you'll do more training," stated Ace.

At the airfield, Ace takes up all the flyers leaving the mechanics and electricians to build the personal hangars underneath the remaining planes. In the air, Ace puts the men through their paces, and he determines which ones to keep as pilots. Back on the ground, Ace approaches one of the mechanics to see if they can come up with a way to slow the speed of the planes once they get to the Zeppelin and match speeds. The next day the Commandant tells the companies that they'll be performing an aerial assault on a Zeppelin at the end of the week, four days from now.

Ace and Bruiser return to the barracks and gives the signal to form up at the South end of the island. Soon Ace's whole company is there in formation. Ace tells them they've only four days left, we'll train up to the third day, and we'll rest on the last night so we can be crisp and ready to do the maneuvers on the Zeppelin.

"We'll be the last ones to take the Zeppelin in this practice. I expect a stellar performance. You all know what you're to do. Get back to your practice. Mechanics and Electricians, how goes the aircraft upgrades?"

"We're just about to be done, and Stan will also finish with the power modifications to slow down the aircraft. We also checked over the aircraft and have selected the ones that were in the best shape."

Ace is not going to fly one of the planes he is going in as an air marine to help subdue the Zeppelin. The big day arrives, and the three companies ahead of Ace's have made their raids, and they each take an hour, give, or take a few minutes. Billy plans to take the Zeppelin in half that time. Ace also realizes that the men aboard the Zeppelin will be ready for his team. So, going through the outer covering of the ship will give Ace and his men an element of surprise instead of using the hangar opening. Each marine is equipped with a knife and rope. Each man will be dropped at a different location along the back of the Zeppelin, and that man will cut the fabric just big enough to pass through, then tie up to the Zeppelin frame and drop down to the maintenance walkway, then proceed to take over the ship. In the thirty minutes, Ace had specified the men reach the bridge of the ship and capture it. The rest of the men they met were put to sleep by the nerve pinches that Ace had taught them to use.

The ship's Captain surrenders his ship, and then Ace and his men make it back up to the outer skin and get picked up by the pilots making their fly byes and scooping up their men for the getaway, which none of the other companies did. They just brought the ship down to the island. Ace's crew could've robbed the Zeppelin and escaped all in the time of one hour. Ace and his company make the best time and get away from the Zeppelin without bringing it to the island. Once again, the Commandant had to pay tribute to Ace's company.

"Since this was a training exercise instead of an actual situation, you may not have succeeded as well as you have," said the Commandant.

Ace is biting his lip. To keep from saying anything. But leave it to Bruiser to open his mouth.

"Sir, we could execute the same thing on a civilian ship. If you don't believe us try us."

"Is that so, Ace?" asks the Commandant.

"Yes, sir, my company can do the same on a civilian ship anytime you want us to."

"Very well, Ace, we'll test it out. It just so happens to be such a vessel flying South of us and will be in range in the next twenty-four hours. Have your men ready we'll observe. How efficient you are."

Ace accepts the challenge. Ace is about to scold Bruiser for speaking up when it dawns on Ace; this'll bring more attention to him and bring him closer to seeing the Queen.

After the award ceremony, Ace collects his men to go over what they had done that day on the Zeppelin; the next one will be for real. Ace has them meet at the South end of the island to discuss what they'll need to do.

"I don't want to kill anyone on this raid, so we need a way to subdue people at a distance. How many air rifles and pistols can we get?"

"What do you want?" asks Bruiser.

"Both, and I want them loaded with sleeping darts, and no one takes a blaster."

"Why do we not want to kill anyone?" asks one of the men.

"Because you cannot rob a dead man a second time, a live

one offers a second opportunity in the future."

"Gotcha! That makes sense," said one of the men.

With the plans, set up Ace has his team check and recheck their equipment.

"We can better our time by flying in formation and dropping the men all at the same time on to the Zeppelin. I'll be in the lead. Now there is one thing to be expecting; I suspect the Commandant will inform the civilian ship that we're coming. Which means the authorities will be ready for us to invade."

"Why'd he do that, Ace? We're Sky Pirates," said one of his men.

"True, but I feel something else is going on, and somehow we're causing a problem to someone else's plans by being better. No one will be a concern if the Sky Pirates are to die in an attempt to rob a civilian Zeppelin", said Ace.

No one else argues with Ace. They've seen how the officers treat them because they are cut better at what they're doing at the training camp, over everyone else.

"Now, based on that assumption, the Zeppelin crew will expect us to attack from the bottom, as they have in the past, and we'll do it from the top, just like we did in our last raid. We get in, and we get out. We take the jewelry money and the cash box with us."

"What about the gold bars?" asks Bruiser?

"We'll leave it, it'll be too heavy to carry, and the jewels will be worth more, so no gold bars, the weight of the jewelry will be heavy enough as it is. Is that clear to everyone?"

"Yes, Sir." they all said.

"To your stations, everyone, we'll be leaving early, like after midnight," stats Ace.

"Ace, the Commandant, said the Zeppelin wouldn't be in position for us until midday," said one of his men.

"I know, think of it this way, have we failed yet as a team?" asks Ace.

"No!" several people said.

"Then we'll do it my way."

"You got it, Ace," said the men.

At midnight, the men meet at the hangar, and Ace and Bruiser have placed the guards watching the hangar and airfield out of commission. They mount up into the planes, take off to the South, and spread out to the point that they can barely see each other, and they sweep the sky looking for the Zeppelin. The man at the farthest sweep point spots the Zeppelin and calls to the rest of the company. Ace has them form up and meet above the Zeppelin in the clouds.

"Ace tells the men (Via Radio) we'll fly out of the Sun down on to the Zeppelin; they won't see us until we began our assault."

Ace passes the signal, and they descend on to the Zeppelin, and everything goes off much as it did the first time, they captured the training Zeppelin. Each man has his target, Ace and two other men make their way to the bridge; when they get there, it has several passengers taking a tour. Ace and his men storm onto the bridge.

Ace tells everyone to raise their hands in the air and to keep their hands visible. Then some guest pulls a blaster, and Ace shoots him with a dart, and the man drops to the deck sound asleep.

"Now is anyone else feeling lucky?" asks Ace. "No, Ok, give us your valuables; the men will collect them."

The men commence to taking valuables from off the passengers. Now Ace and his men are wearing the Sky Pirate uniforms with a mask, so they'd not be recognized. Ace runs on to a couple; she is as young as he is, with honey-colored hair and black highlights and a man he knows as Captain Rogers from the Zeppelin that transported him to the island.

Ace is polite and asks the two to contribute to him and his men, the woman does so, but the man starts to struggle, when Ace gives him a neck pinch, dropping him on to the floor, where Ace searches him and takes his belongings. The whole time the girl watches and doesn't flinch one bit.

"Did you kill him?" she asks.

"No, he's alive, but will have a bad headache when he does wake."

"Too bad, he's such a bore."

"Bloodthirsty, aren't you?" said Ace.

"It comes with the territory. What's your name?"

"Not on the first date," said Ace.

Ace turns to the Captain of this Zeppelin and robs him, and during the process, Ace uses sleight of hand to passes a note to the Zeppelin's Captain to contact the Secret Police and tell them Ace is moving up in the ranks.

One of the passengers is watching Ace and sees that he has passed the Captain a note. He also noticed that Ace had put all the Captain's things back in another pocket. When Ace and his men leave, the man bumps into the Captain and takes the note. Then returns in his cabin, the man (Secret Policeman) reads the note, contacts his superiors, and relays the message. The Secret Police officer then returns to following the Sky Pirate Princess to get to the Queen.

Ace and his men depart the Zeppelin and return to the island, where a squad of men waits to arrest them. Ace turns over the loot they'd taken and then convinces the Commandant that he's the one to blame, not his men. They let them go as they arrest Ace for not following orders. While in his cell, the Commandant receives communication from the Sky Pirate Princess. She orders that the men who raided the Zeppelin to be sent to the Island fortress, immediately, and the Commandant will be held responsible if the men and the leader fail to appear. Shaken, the Commandant arranges to have the men confined to their barracks along with Ace. A few days, The Zeppelin docks on the island and Ace with his company are put on board, then placed in protective custody where they cannot see where they're going. They're treated well for the whole trip, but no one will talk with them.

On the third day, they land on an island with a fortress up on a mountain. Ace and his men are led off the Zeppelin and told to follow the path to the castle. Ace leads his men, and they march up to the castle gates. Ace forms up his men, and they stand at the closed entrance for an hour. Then, the entrance is opened, and a squad of men with weapons surrounds Ace, and his men then escort them into the castle. Off to the right is dais where sits a beautiful woman in some regal dress, with assorted cronies surrounding her. Ace forms up his men again and salutes the Queen.

"Young man, do you know who I am?"

"From all the secrecy, I'd assume you're the Sky Pirate leader," states Ace.

"You're quite right, young man I am the Sky Pirate Queen."

"My men and I stand ready to serve you then," said Ace.

"Young man, what is your name?"

"Ace Williams, just Ace."

"Well, Ace Williams, I knew of another person named Webber from years ago, and he turned out to be a spy.

Anyone, you know perhaps? You do seem to match his appearance though somewhat younger."

"I wouldn't know, your highness my father died when I was very young, and my mother died when I was eighteen, I've been on my own all that time."

"Don't be coy, Mr. Ace Webber, I have everybody investigated completely, and I know your real name. It appears your last name is the same as William Webber. Have I let another spy into my midst?" the Queen asks.

"No, mam! Just a man who needs a place in this world or rather a place to fit into."

"That remains to be seen, young man, be assured that you'll be watched and listened to."

"Yes, mam," acknowledges Ace.

"Now tell me about the raid on the Zeppelin, I hear you managed to pull it off without killing anyone," commands the Queen.

"We did take the Zeppelin without killing anyone. I don't know how much loot we got away with. When we returned to base, we were arrested."

The Queen waves away that part of the report as if it were unimportant. Then from beside the throne out steps, the girl he met on the Zeppelin and beside her Captain Rogers of the pirate's Zeppelin that had taken him to the training base island and who tried to get him killed with the Fleet-Champion.

"Tell me, young man, would you be willing to demonstrate your fighting style to these people and me if I ask it of thee?"

"Whatever your highness wishes," answers Ace.

"Good, pick another of your men, and I'll pit you against two of my champions of choice. Tonight then? Chamberlin set it up for after the evening meal."

"Yes, your highness."

"Chamberlin, see to these men and get them situated."

"Yes, your majesty."

Ace and his men are led to the backside of the castle and provided a barracks to settle in; the Chamberlin tells Ace where he and his men can go to get chow.

"You'd best get some rest, your fight later will be dangerous, and you'll want to be well-rested, I'll come and get you when it's time."

"Thank you, Chamberlin," said Ace.

Ace tells Bruiser that he'll be fighting with him tonight and remember all that he's been taught. Don't lose your temper. Ace turns in to get some sleep from the long flight. Then two hours before the Chamberlin is to come and get Ace and Bruiser. Ace and Bruiser are up stretching and doing some warm-up exercises. When the Chamberlin arrives, he sees the two men being cheered on by the rest of the company.

"If you two are ready, it's time to go." states the Chamberlin.

Billy and Bruiser fall in to step with the Chamberlin and are taken to a ring where they are to fight. Ace and Bruiser enter the ring and are announced as rookies, and then the other two men approach they are announced as the Queen's Champions. Ace sizes up the competition.

"Bruiser, we have the advantage."

"How's that Ace, they look pretty mean even to me."

"Look how they move. They're much like you were when

we met, we can use that against the champions."

"I get it, yea!" said Bruiser.

"Bruiser, don't get mad, and you can beat them."

The fight starts, and Ace takes on one opponent and Bruiser the other. The match only lasts one round to the disappointment of the assembled guests. Both of the Queen's champions are knocked out, neither Ace nor Bruiser take the laurels for winning the fight since the champions knocked themselves out. By being thrown into each other headfirst. Ace and Bruiser are returned to the barracks. As Ace and Bruiser are getting ready to turn in for the night. The Chamberlin barges into the barracks.

"The Queen wants to have an audience with you two, so get dressed," commands the Chamberlin.

Ace and Bruiser dress in their uniforms and soon find themselves standing in front of the Queen, and they bow to her.

"You requested our presents, your majesty," asked Ace.

"Quite so, you bested my best fighters; it appears without much effort. You'll protect me at the banquet tomorrow night!"

Bowing, "We'd be honored to guard your person at the banquet, your majesty." said Ace

"Then, you shall!" The Queen then waves them off.

Ace and Bruiser take a few steps back bowing at each step, then do a crisp turn to leave the Queen's chambers. Elsewhere in the lower part of the castle, Captain Rogers is talking to a mysterious man known only as the assassin, the assassin's face is covered.

"Tomorrow night is the banquet; you'll kill the Queen during the meal," demands Captain Rogers.

"That shouldn't be a problem, what's the payment?"

"What we agreed upon, and only if you don't get caught."

"I've never been caught, and I'll not be noticed until I'm gone," stated the assassin.

"They have some rookies guarding the Queen that should make it easy for you," said Captain Rogers.

"Good, then you should have nothing to worry about, have my payment ready for me; I'll want to leave right after I've completed my task."

"I'll have it for you at the cove where we first met," noted Captain Rogers.

"Be sure that you do, or you'll be the next target."

The assassin walks off into the dark. Moments later, the Commandant from the island walks up to Captain Rogers, "is it all set?"

"Yes, with Ace and his team watching over the Queen at the banquet; when she's assassinated, the whole lot will be executed for dereliction of duty. I'll force the Princess to marry me so I can take over the Sky Pirate organization."

"I'll say you have this well planned out, Captain."

"One other thing, I'll need one other person taken care of?"

"Who might that be, Captain?"

"The assassin, of course."

"Yes Captain, it'll be done, I'll have a sniper in position."

Both men go their separate ways. The next morning the Captain boards his Zeppelin and takes off to take care of an issue on the training island, so he'll not be at the banquet when the Queen is assassinated so that he can divert suspicion from himself. The assassin locates the headwaiter and kills him so he can take his place. The killer hides the dead waiter in the dungeon out of sight. Then he takes his clothes and even makes up his face to look a lot like the headwaiter. Then he goes up to the kitchen and checks the layout. The assassin tries out his appearance with the other kitchen staff. He manages to pass himself off as the headwaiter without too much problem. The killer returns to the dungeon, to make sure the real waiter hasn't been found, and his shoes pick up some dirt from the dungeon floor.

That night the banquet is being held, the assassin places himself at the doorway into the dining hall so he can inspect all the food trays taken out to the guests. Ace and his men are not used to the formal way of eating, but for the most part, all they have to do is stand at attention, look sharp, and keep an eye out for trouble. Ace stands to the left side of the Queen and can see the door to the kitchen, and he considers the headwaiter as he looks at the food and drinks coming out of the kitchen. Ace is disturbed by something, the way the headwaiter is acting, doesn't seem right. Ace walks up to the waiter and asks what the next entree is to be served next. Ace notices that the waiter hesitates in his answer, and Ace looks down at the waiter's shoes and says nothing, but returns to his station next to the Queen.

When the meal is over and drinks are being dispensed when Ace sees the waiter pull a blowgun from his sleeve, Ace roughly takes the drink tray from a passing server causing all the drinks to spill and then uses the tray to deflect the dart the assassin shot at the Queen. Then using the tray as a weapon, Ace hurls the tray at the assassin and hits him on the bridge of the nose knocking him to the ground, causing a ruckus with the staff and the guests. Ace and Bruiser subdue the assassin. The Queen comes over to see the man.

"Ah, so you were to kill me tonight, who put you up to it?" the Queen demands.

The assassin makes no reply. Ace decides to persuade him. By pinching a nerve bundle at the back of the assassin's neck, the killer screams. Ace stops the pain.

"Answer the Queen, or I'll apply the pain again." No answer, Ace applies the pinch again, and the assassin screams in pain Ace lets it last longer this time.

"Who put you up to killing the Queen?"

Still no answer, Ace applies the pinch a third time when the assassin is shot out of nowhere and dies. The Princess enters the room, from a stroll with one of the other officers.

"Mother, are you hurt?" she asks.

"No, my dear, this young man protected me, and the assassin is now dead shot by some unknown assailant. From up on the balcony."

The Princess looks Ace over. "This is twice you have saved me, sir. Once on the Zeppelin from Captain Rogers, and now my mother from an assassin. Thank You!"

Ace bows to her, "No need to thank me, your highness, I was just doing my duty."

One of the kitchen staff hurries into the banquet room, "we've found the headwaiter; he's dead and in one of the last cells in the dungeon," said one of the servers.

"I want to know who tried to kill me. I want this island searched, no one is to leave or land on the island without my permission," commands the Queen.

Ace tells his men to stay close to the Queen. And to escort her to her rooms, and guard her against harm. With the Queen in her chambers. A comprehensive search is made to find who shot the assassin. The Chamberlin locates the place where the shot came from. It's from an upper balcony, near a tapestry. Ace and Bruiser look along the balcony area, inspecting the walls and floor when Bruiser leans against a tapestry and falls through an opening. Letting out a yelp as he falls. Ace returns to Bruiser. "Are you alright, Bruiser?"

"I'm fine; I think I found where the killer entered and left the balcony. Ouch!" as he rubs a sore arm.

"Good Job Bruiser, let's see where it leads."

Ace and Bruiser grab a torch and follow the passage, at first, it's level then it leads down some stairs, with a few twists and turns leading to the bottom of the castle not far from the water surrounding the island. They spot footprints in the wet sand, and so they follow them. The prints take them around the North end of the island, to a secluded place.

"Hey, Ace, do you hear that? A plane is getting ready to take off."

"Let's hurry, Bruiser we might be able to catch them." Shouts Ace.

Ace and Bruiser drop the torch and run flat out toward the noise of the plane. As they round the point, they can see one of the aircraft fitted for landing on the water taking off, and in a short time, it's lost in the darkness as it flies out to sea.

"Looks like we lost him, Bruiser, we'd better report back to the Queen."

"Right behind you, Ace."

12

"Well kids it's time for a break, Grandpa needs to get up and get something to eat and drink, anyone else wants to join me?"

"Sure, Dad," as his son turns off the recording device and follows dad into the house.

After a repast and some lemonade, everyone reconvenes at the picnic table to continue the story of Billy Webber and the Sky Pirates.

"Now let me see, where did I leave off?"

"Grandpa, Billy, and Bruiser are heading back to see the Queen," said Jeff.

Ace and Bruiser return by the way they'd left the castle and find a contingent of the Queen's men on the balcony. "The man who shot the assassin has fled off the island; we need to tell the Queen," announces Ace.

The Queen's men form up around Ace and Bruiser to escort them to the Queen's chamber. The Queen has changed out of her formal wear and into something less gaudy; her daughter is there as well.

"Well, young man, explain yourself!" demands the Queen.

"How do you mean your majesty," asks Ace.

"I told you to escort me to my chambers, and you had your men do that while you ran off, explain your actions."

"Your Majesty, I was in pursuit of the man who shot the assassin, and we almost caught up to him. He used a secret passage from the balcony that leads down to the sea. Bruiser and I were just about to catch up to him; he flew off in a plane that was waiting for him. He got away."

"I see; did you see who it was?" she demanded.

"No, Bruiser, and I couldn't make him out in the dark. Your Majesty may I ask you some questions?" Ace requests.

"My, you are impertinent one, aren't you, young man?"

"Yes, mam," says Ace.

"Ask your questions, if I choose, I'll answer."

"If you were removed from the throne, who'd take over the Sky Pirates?"

"My Daughter here would. Are you saying she is trying to have me killed?"

"Would she not?" queries Ace.

"What do you mean by that remark?" said the Queen sternly.

"Who in this organization would stand the most to gain if you and your daughter were removed from ruling?" asked Ace.

"That'd fall to Captain Rogers, why? He's the most trusted man that is under me."

"I wonder?" muses Ace.

"Enough! Everyone, please put your hands in the air." As Captain Rogers steps from a hidden wall panel waving an energy blaster.

Holding the blaster on everyone, "Continue, Ace, tell us more about this conspiracy," said Captain Rogers.

"The way I see it, you get the Queen killed, then you force the daughter to be your wife, or you kill her, and take over as King of the Sky Pirates," said Ace.

"Excellent, Ace, now!" A dart is stuck in Captain Roger's cheek; he drops his gun and falls to the floor, paralyzed.

"Good shot, Vantessa. Ace you and your men take this trader down into the dungeon, I want to have a chat with him," says the Queen.

Ace and a few of his men pick up Captain Rogers, and carry him to the dungeon and put him into a cell. At the Queen's command, they tie up his hands and feet, and the Queen sticks another dirt into Roger's hand to counter the first drug that paralyzed him.

"Now Captain, start talking, who're the others with you in this conspiracy?" commands the Queen.

"I won't tell," squeaks Captain Rogers.

"You will, Roger dear, you will. Ace get that fire going, some hot iron will loosen his tongue." chuckles the Queen.

Ace walks over to Captain Roger's and pinches his neck, and Rogers starts screaming, after a few moments, Ace pinches his neck again, and the pain stops. "I'd recommend you answer her Captain, or I'll do it again."

"No! I won't tell you." Ace pinches his neck again, and the Captain starts screaming again. Then Ace gets up to leave, when between the screams, "I'll talk." Ace stops the pain. Captain Rogers starts to talk when an energy bolt kills him. Everyone looks up, and a man of middle years walks through the cell door with a blaster in his hand. The Queen's eyes got huge at seeing him.

"Victor, my son?" said the Queen in surprise.

"Why, yes, mother, dear, it's me."

"It can't be, you're…"

"Oh, you mean dead. The news of my death is a bit premature mother. I must admit, though, I would've been dead if not for the intervention of William Webber. All those years ago, he spirited me away from my room before it blew up. Too bad that I had to blow him up after he saved me and all. I couldn't have anyone know that I was still alive. So, I left a bomb in his plane, and it killed him."

Ace's feelings about his dad's death, almost made Ace forget why he was there in the first place, it was to bring down the Sky Pirates, not kill his father's killer.

"Victor, what are you planning to do now?" asks the Queen.

"Why mother, your death, of course. Although I can assure you, I wasn't part of the conspiracy; I'll have to root out the others after I consolidate my position," smirked Victor.

Before anyone can move, Victor kills his mother with a shot to her head. Then he backs out of the cell and locks it.

"I'll be back to finish the job, once I have my sister secured or dead," said Victor.

"We're in a tough spot now, Ace, with that psycho, waiting to come back and kill us."

Ace frisks the Captain and the Queen and finds a key on

her person.

"Ace, how'd you know she had a key?" questions Bruiser.

"I didn't, I was hoping, and so far, we lucked out."

Ace tried the door, and the key unlocked it. "Now Bruiser go around up the boys, and I'll try to rescue the Princess.

"Will you need any help, Ace?" asks Bruiser.

"No, I have a score to settle, I'll be just fine." Ace said with conviction.

They separate, and Bruiser heads to the barracks to collect the men. Then back to the castle to locate the Princess. Ace soon discovers the room where the Princess is, from all the screaming; Ace gets there and peeks around the corner to see what's happening. Victor has his sister's arm and is trying to lead her out of her room.

"Come on, sis, if you don't, I'll kill you as I did them." Victor points his gun at the men on the floor, with blaster holes in various places.

"No!" she screams. "Let me go!"

"Oh well, then." He turns her loose and draws a bead on her forehead. "Goodbye, sis."

As he is about to pull the trigger, Ace shoots him in the neck with a sleep dart, and Victor drops to the floor paralyzed. Ace walks up and removes his blaster, and the Princess runs to his side.

"Where's mother?" she asks.

"I'm sorry Victor here killed her before I could do anything to save her."

At the door, several men of Ace's company enter the Queen's Bedroom, where Ace and the Princess are standing over Victor. Ace turns to one of his men.

"Tie him up and find a cell for him, he has a lot to answer for," states Ace.

"Victor is the rightful heir to the throne," said the Princess.

"Do you know for sure he's Victor?" asks Ace.

"Yes, he's Victor, and the rightful King of the Sky Pirates," claims the Princess.

"Until I can sort all this out, I'm going to declare martial law, men escort the Princess to her room, and guard her there," said Ace.

Ace finds himself in a position of stopping the Sky Pirates forever. Ace returns to the barracks and locates his transponder. Ace puts it into his pocket, then stalks out of the building into the courtyard. Ace then turns and walks down into the dungeon to talk with Victor. When Ace arrives, Victor is awake and alert.

"Oh, good, you can answer some questions for me," says Ace.

"Why should I do that?" sneers Victor.

"If you want to get out of this cell, you might want to consider, that the reason," warns Ace.

Victor looks into Ace's eyes, and stairs for some moments then nods his head yes.

"Now you can see Victor; I don't care if you're King here or not, I don't care who rules the Sky Pirates. Now answer the questions. Why'd you choose this time to return here?"

"My sister, Vantessa, sent me a message, telling me it was time to make my bid for the throne, that all the players were here and in place for me to dispose of, and then take my rightful place here as the King."

"Your sister the Princess?" said Ace in an astonished voice.

"Quite so old boy, my sister. You see, she's good at playing games. She's the one who gave Captain Rogers the idea to become King, and then let all chips fall where they may. I'd not be surprised if dear sister set up the assassination attempt on dear old mom."

"If no one knew you were alive or where you were, how did your sister find you?" asks Ace.

"Some years ago, while learning to be a farmer and a fisherman. A Sky Pirate came to our island. Like so many of the people, we all went to gawk at him. For some reason, he stopped next to me and looked at me, not saying a word. He then got into his plane and took off. Several months later he returns, and looks me up and gives me a letter from my sister. So, we corresponded secretly for a few years. Then I got a letter a month ago. Come all is set up for you to take over as King."

"I see, I was almost right, the one who'd benefit the most would be the new Queen."

"No old boy, the new King."

"No Victor, you have it all wrong. She's going to have you killed so that she can take over as Queen."

"What! She is going to kill me!"

"Quite so old boy," smirks Ace.

"You can't let her do that; you have to protect me," screams Victor.

"I don't, I've never sworn fealty to any of you, and so you are not my King. Now I'll see your sister. Bruiser, please get in here."

Bruiser walks in. "Yes, Ace?"

"Guard this man until further notice. No one is to get in here but me."

"Yes, Sir."

Ace heads to the Princesses' rooms to have a chat with her. Ace knocks on the door and is asked to enter. Ace enters the room and sees his two men there with the Princess sitting in a chair.

"Your brother is interesting to talk to; did you know that?" queries Ace.

"What'd Victor say? That all this is my fault or my idea?" said the Princess with some heat in her voice.

"Something like that, all I want to know is, is it true?"

"What do you think?" spat out the Princess.

"I don't know what to think, Princess; given your family, I feel you truly could be that ruthless."

"You may leave my presents, Sir," demands the Princess.

Ace leaves her room and walks out to the central courtyard and sets off the transponder, to call in the Secret Police so that they can clean up this nest of intrigue. Ace isn't sure of how long the Police will take to arrive. In the meantime, he has to run this place. Ace decides to place the Princess under protective custody and to keep her brother in his cell in the dungeon.

"Ace, why don't you take over the Sky Pirates you'd make a good leader," said Bruiser.

"Not me, I have enough things in my life to keep me busy, and besides, I like my freedom. Being a King means giving up your freedom to serve others and always being responsible. That's not for me Bruiser, serving in this capacity suits me, and in the end, I can walk away and be my own man."

"I see, the boys and I were just suggesting. We'd all follow you without question."

"Thanks, Bruiser, I hope that remains true when all this is over, and we can go back to being who we were."

"Ace, what are we going to do, for now, keep everyone here until. Someone with authority arrives to take charge."

"That's what we're going to do, Bruiser. Keep an eye on the two prisoners and make sure they don't escape, and they're taken care of. Keep at least two people at all times with The Princess, make sure she is especially watched. She is more dangerous than her brother."

"I will, Ace," said Bruiser.

Bruiser walks off to follow Ace's orders, and Ace is left alone with his thoughts. (I hope the Police get here soon.) Ace takes a walk to get away from the turmoil. As he walks along the beach, he finds a boat, already to sail off. Ace climbs aboard, disconnects the motor, continues his walk, and arrives at the small airfield. Ace does the same to all the planes. He goes behind the hangar and buries the parts he has taken. Just to be sure, Ace continues his walk around the island. In a hidden cove, he finds a water plane. Ace disables it for good measure, and he buries the parts nearby at the base of a tree then Ace returns to the castle.

When Ace gets there, everyone is on alert and running to battle stations. Ace stops one of the men.

"What's going on here? What's all the fuss?"

"The Secret Police have found us and are about to land; we need direction, are you now in charge?"

"Yes, call everyone into formation without guns." Commands Ace.

"But Sir, the Police will arrest us."

"Do as I say!" snapped Ace.

"Yes, Sir."

Ace assembles all the men except for the ones guarding the prisoners.

"Men, if you'll trust me, I'll take care of you all."

"Sir, these are the Secret Police, they'll jail us and throw away the key. Said one man".

"Ok, I understand, but you must trust me, ask the men that came with me, I always have a plan if you'll follow me. I'll take care of you. At worse, we'll all go to jail for a short time. Will that not be better than for the rest of your life?" asks Ace.

The men grumble but agree. Soon the Police storm the castle with weapons drawn, and the men are in formation standing at attention. Ace steps up and announces to the Police that no resistance will be given. The officer in charge binds Ace in handcuffs and carts him off.

"That was the easiest bust we've ever made, Billy, thanks," said the Commander.

"You are welcome, Sir. Please let me put in a good word for the men, and I'll turn over the Princess and Prince of the Sky Pirates, they're the guilty ones. Both have killed while the men that you currently have; haven't."

"Ok, Billy, we can do that," said the commander.

"Thanks," said Billy, "now follow me."

Billy leads the Police to the dungeon to arrest the prince of the Sky Pirates. Once shackled and under guard, they lead him away to the waiting Zeppelin. Then Billy leads the officer to the Princess's chambers. Upon entering, they find all four men dead, and the Princess is gone.

"How?" was all Billy asked. Billy checked the walls there must be a hidden compartment, looking at the floor Billy finds the wall she went through. Rather than try to open it, Billy guides the Police out the gate and heads to the secret cove where the plane was all ready to fly away. When they arrive, they hear cursing that would make a sailor proud.

"My, my, such language from a Princess no less," said Billy.

"You! You're a traitor; you did all this, did you not?" more a statement than a question.

"Yes, I did," said Billy.

"Why?" Vantessa asked.

"You killed my parents, my father, and years later, my mother. Officer, please taker her away. Be careful she is very dangerous," warns Billy.

The Police shackle her arms and legs. Then escort Vantessa to the Zeppelin, and place her in a cell across from her brother.

"Well, Sister, I see we both share the same accommodations," and he starts laughing.

"Brother I'd not get too happy about it, they plan on stretching our necks, I told you to wait, but you had to execute your take over too soon. If you'd have waited, you'd have been the King as I promised."

"Yes, for how long, sister, a day maybe. You were planning

on killing me soon afterward, were you not?" spat Victor.

"Whatever my plans, dear brother, they're not likely to happen. Now, are they dear brother?"

"I think what's rich is that you fell for the very guy who put us here,' laughs the prince.

"Don't crow so much brother; I have a plan."

"What might that be, sis?"

"You'll have to wait, brother."

Chapter

13

Billy is in the Commander's office, trying to spring his men from jail.

"Look, Commander, if not for the men I recruited to help me, you'd not have captured the Sky Pirates, so I'm asking you to release them into my custody. They'll come around and want to join the Secret Police. I can guarantee they'll be among the best men that you have."

"Ok, Mr. Webber, but only after we land at the base, I'll take no chances with the rest."

"Yes, Sir!" Billy salutes the Commander, does a quick turn, and leaves the office. Billy turns up at the brig moments later.

"Get out of here, traitor!" says Bruiser and the men with him."

"Guys, listen. I just talked to the Commander, when we land at the base, you're to be turned over to me, and you'll be trained as Secret Police, under my command. I reminded the Commander that if it were not for you guys, they'd not have captured the Sky Pirates."

"We followed you, Ace; now look where it got, us," stated Bruiser.

"Please, listen; we've forged a good team. We work well together, and we've accomplished a lot together. We still can, all I'm asking of you is to become Police, instead of crooks. By the way, Bruiser, you'll be my second in command. What do you say? Just think it over; you'll have about a day before we land." Pleads Billy

That night, the Princess Vantessa puts her plan to work, and at midnight a Secret Police guard comes to check on the prisoners. He opens the cell door of the Princess and strips out of his clothes, and the Princess strips out of her clothes. The Princess dresses in the guard's clothes, and he dresses in hers. Vantessa exits her cell. She crosses to her brother's cell and wakes him up.

"Brother, wake up," whispers Vantessa.

Her brother stirs and sits up, then he sees her at his cell door, and he comes up to her.

"Let me out of here." He commands.

"Sure, thing, brother." Vantessa pulls a knife and stabs Victor through the bars right in the heart.

"I wanted you to see that I have escaped brother before you die." spits Vantessa.

The Princess makes her way to the bottom of the Zeppelin where a plane hangs in a cradle, she gets in and fires up the engine, and then drops the aircraft in a free fall and flies off toward an island where she plans to hide for a short time then return to the castle for some money.

Food arrives for the Princess and the Prince. The Police

discover the deception. The death of the prince. The Commander initiates a search; of the Zeppelin. To locate Vantessa, and after a time, they find the plane missing from its cradle. The Commander calls Billy to his office.

"This is embarrassing, Billy; we have to catcher her again."

"I can capture her, but I need the help of my men that you hold in the brig."

"All alright, release them, but I'll hold you responsible for their actions," said the Commander.

"You won't be sorry, Commander. By the way, the man that replaced the Princess, where is he, I'd like to have a chat with him."

"He's dead; he took poison shortly after we discovered the deception."

"Ok, I guess we'll have to do this the hard way." Billy squares his shoulders and goes to the brig, to recruit his men.

"Men, you've been released into my custody, I need your help to recapture the Princess."

"Why should we care?" asks one of the men.

"Look, I've done all that I can to get you out of here so you can be free men, so either you follow me or rot in prison. Your choice. Now who's with me?" asks Billy.

At first, no one moves or says anything, and then Bruiser speaks up. "I'll follow you, Ace, either as a pirate or policeman."

Soon the others join in, and then his whole company joins him.

"Thank you, men; you make me proud of all of you. Now let's put an end to the Sky Pirates."

The men fall into formation. And follow Billy out of the brig into the barracks the Commander gave to Billy and his men.

"Here are some civilian clothes to wear; you'll all be undercover. When you find the Princess don't try to capture her, she is deadly and merciless, repot back to Bruiser here who'll be in the command center."

"But Ace, I want to go with you!"

"Bruiser, I need you here, the men respect you and trust you, so do I. If anyone gets so, much as a lead, I want to know about it. We'll be touching down in one hour be ready to leave."

"Ace, where're you going?" questions Bruiser.

"Back to the island, I suspect she'll want to reclaim the throne, and I'd not be surprised if there are still a few secrets that it still holds. I'm going to visit a friend of mine so I can get my plane. I'll need it to catch her," said Billy.

"Ok, Ace, but be careful and return, I don't want to be a policeman without you to keep me in line," said Bruiser, shaking Billy's hand.

Billy shakes Bruiser's hand. "I'll be back, if for no other reason than to keep you in line," smiles Billy.

Billy takes one of the planes at the base airfield and flies back home to his hangar, where he stored his plane before going on assignment, and to see an old friend. In one's day, time Billy makes it back to his hangar and pulls his aircraft out of storage. As he is working on getting his plane ready, his next-door neighbor enters Billy's hangar to see why it's all lit up. When he sees Billy, Jim is so excited they have a tearful reunion. Then Jim pitches in and helps Billy to get his plane ready to fly. When the plane is prepared, Jim invites Billy to his house for dinner, and Billy accepts. The whole night is spent in Billy telling Jim all that has happened, and that he's now on the trail of the Sky Pirate Princess Vantessa to bring her to justice. Having finished his story, Billy drifts off to sleep on the couch, and Jim covers him in a blanket. Jim stands there looking down at Billy when Jim's wife comes up to him and stands beside him.

"They grow up fast, don't they Jim?" she whispers.

"Yes, dear, they do, Children one day then grownups the next. In Billy's case, much too fast. I hope one day he'll find a pretty girl like you dear and will settle down and have children."

The couple leaves the room to let Billy sleep the morning away. Billy awakes to hear a conversation coming from the kitchen and so he enters it to find Jim and his wife at the table, sharing a coffee and cakes.

"Billy, would you like something to eat?"

"Yes, Please."

"Here, sit down, and I'll get you some bacon and eggs."

"That would be great, Mrs. Collins."

Billy pours a coffee for himself and has a conversation with Jim while he waits for breakfast. "That girl that used to come to my hangar, how's she doing?"

"She got married, and her first child is on the way. Would you like me to take you to her?"

"No, Jim, I wouldn't, and I'm sure her husband wouldn't like it either."

"You're probably right, Billy," said Jim.

Breakfast arrives, and Billy eats it all with a great deal of enthusiasm, you'd think the man hadn't eaten in a long time. When Billy finished, he complimented Mrs. Collins and threatened to steal her form Jim, making her laugh, and blush at the same time.

"Well it's time to go, I've a Princess to catch and put behind bars."

Jim drives Billy to the airfield and drops him at his hangar; Billy gets into his plane and taxies down the taxi away, then lines up on the runway and takes off into the next part of his adventure.

"Well, guys, it's dark, and I see your Big sister is sound asleep, and that Jeff is not far behind. Let's call it a night, and we can pick up again tomorrow morning."

Colleen picks up Cindy, and Doug picks up Jeff and carries them into the house to put them to bed. Everyone turns in for the night. In the morning after a hearty breakfast, they all adjourn at the patio table to listen to Grandpa continue the story of Billy Webber and the Sky Pirates.

Grandpa scratches at his chin and looks upward as if in contemplation so he can collect his thoughts before he launched back into his story.

"Let me see, oh yes, I watch and wave as Billy takes off in pursuit of the Princess; he flies back to the coast to see if he can pick up a trail of where she may have landed. "

After her escape, the Princess stops in one of the roughest bars in the area in hopes of picking up a few rather bad men. The Princess enters the bar, and the men are rough-looking, just the type she needs. When she explains that she is the Princess of the Sky Pirates, the men all laugh at her. A large man grabs the Princess and throws her on to a table. Planning to have his way with her. At first, she puts up a fight and then relaxes as the man leans closer to her to tell her what he plans to do to her. She grabs his neck and pinches the nerve centers causing him to fall to the floor in great pain, she gets up and stands next to him, and he grabs her leg, and she kicks him in the face, "what were you going to do to me?" the man continues to writhe in pain. He gasps out, "Please make it stop!"

"Lay there and grovel, you uncouth bustard! Now is there anyone else who wants to sample my charms? No takers. Good! Now back to my question. Who'll follow me and become a Sky Pirate?"

Some of the men scoff at her, and others go and stand behind her. Just you few. She draws her blaster and kills the ones who don't join her. Then she turns to the man writhing on the floor, are you going to join me. He does all he can to give her his ascent that he'll join her. The Princess touches his neck, and the pain stops.

"Now, get up! We need to get some transportation to a distant island. What does this place have to offer by way of transportation?" demands Princess Vantessa.

One of the men says there's a small Zeppelin at the hangar; we could steal that for transportation. The Princess looks at him and smiles.

"Well, men, what're we waiting for, move out," commands Vantessa.

They get to the airfield, and the Princess helps the men

capture the Zeppelin, and she takes the plane she flew in on, with the secret police emblem on it, and puts it on board the Zeppelin. With the idea to repaint it later.

One of the men came to the Princess, "who knows how to fly this ship, none of us do."

"Don't worry, boys; I can fly this ship, now get on board. Now which of you is a mechanic?" asks the Princess.

The man she had writhing in agony said he was one.

"Good I want you to go over that plane and remove the locator beacons it has, and quickly."

"Yes, Princess."

The Princess heads to the bridge, "you two come with me, and we're going to get off the ground now."

She places one man on the helm, and the other at the radar station, she fires up the engines and guides the ship out of the hangar as if she were a seasoned flyer, once out she takes them into the sky, at an altitude of about ten thousand feet where they level out.

Helm turn the wheel to port and "bring us about to two-o-Five degrees, and stay on that heading until I tell you differently," commands Vantessa.

"Yes! Princess."

The Princess decides to look over the rest of the men to see what she has; after all, you can only do so much with six men. She'll need to find others to join them. To do that, she is headed back to the island where the training facility is to see if any other men have escaped the Secret Police. If no one is there, she'll go to other places to recruit her men and maybe some women, if they can measure up to her standards.

At the same time, Billy is winging his way to the location where the Princess landed; he follows the locator beacon on the plane she took. It takes Billy a couple of more days to reach the settlement when he arrives, he finds that the town is in mourning. Billy asks around, and he hears the story about a woman who showed up to recruit men for Sky Pirates, and the ones who choose not to join were gunned down in cold blood. Billy discovers that they stole a small Zeppelin and flew off; she mentioned a remote island. Not much help there, there are a lot of remote islands on this planet called Topaz. Billy returns to his plane and tries to locate the plane she took from the Secret Police, and he gets one blip and then it dies. At least he has a heading. Billy figures she'll head to the island where the Sky Pirates were being trained.

Billy purchases some food and water then set off in the direction of the last blip he had picked up. Billy is going to follow the Princess to the training island. It's three long days of flying without a stop. Billy is running out of food and water, and the worst thing he is getting tired and it's getting hard to stay awake. He almost crashed into a massive wave as he fell asleep at the stick. Billy wakes just in time to climb back up to a safer height. On the evening of the third day, Billy spots an island and decides to make a landing. Once on the ground, all Billy can think of is getting some sleep. Billy crawls under his plane and falls fast asleep. Billy sleeps well into the late morning. When he wakes up, he realizes he is hungry and thirsty. Billy explores the island and finds a spring not far away, and Billy fills his canteen. A Big further on, Billy runs on to a bird's nest with three eggs, so he removes them and eats them raw.

Billy realizes this is not the island he's looking for, a matter of fact it's deserted, Billy decides to get back into the air. After checking over his plane, Billy mounts up and flies off the island. Billy takes his original heading and flies on in search of the Princess. Billy flies past two more islands when he spots the Sky Pirate training base, he drops low and sees a Zeppelin moored at the hangar. Billy decides that landing at the South end of the island will give him a better chance to sneak up on the main offices and see what the Princess is up too.

Chapter

15

Billy lands his plane and takes the time to cover it with brush, so it'll not be seen from the air. Billy travels overland to the training camp. Billy surveys the area and sees about twelve people not counting the Princess. Billy can move about unseen for the most part. One of the places Billy invades is the supply hut. He finds a bag and fills it with food and water. Billy then returns to his plane to set up a camp of sorts. The food he took will not have to be cooked, so no fire. Billy breaks in the supply hut again the next day to get some blankets and more water.

Billy decides to see what's in the armory but finds it a bit more challenging to enter the building. Billy doesn't want to alert anyone to his presents, so he doesn't attack the guard. He waits until dark when they change the guards. Billy watches, and soon the guard becomes complacent, and sits down and promptly falls asleep. Billy sneaks up to him and makes sure he stays asleep. Once inside the supply hut Billy rummages around looking for explosives, ammo, and a few blasters. Billy puts what he finds into his bag, and then he carefully mines the place with the rest of the explosives. Billy shoulders his bag and starts to leave the building when he remembers the man just outside the door.

As Billy leaves, he drags the man out of harm's way, and heads for the dense brush, at a safe distance Billy, triggers a remote detonator, and the armory goes up in a terrible explosion.

The Princess shows up to the burning building.

"What happened?" She asked the man she placed in charge.

"We don't know yet; Private Phillips was on duty."

"Well, he had better be dead, or he will be," stated the Princess.

"Phillip is here, Princess."

"Bring him to me! Now Phillip, what happened?" demands the Princess.

"I don't know; I was guarding the armory, then everything went black, until now. I saw no one, and I heard nothing."

In her anger, the Princess pulls a blaster and kills Phillip.

"If anyone gets caught sleeping at his post, he'll also get the same execution as Phillips just did. Now find out who did this. I want every inch of this island searched, and bring me the man who did this!" and the Princess stalks off to the building she is using as her quarters.

On her way to her *quarters, the Princess muses about whom it might be who caused this explosion; she realizes that it might be Billy; only he'd move a man from danger. He'll have to be dealt with, too bad that, I rather like him. I've even considered making him my*

Billy heard the order and decided to return to his plane and get off this island. Upon returning to his aircraft, Billy locates a tall tree and climbs up to place a transponder to bring the Secret Police. Once he has the transponder going, he uncovers his plane, as Billy is about to board.

"Hands up, and don't move," says one of the men.

Billy does as he's told; one of the two men takes his blaster. Then ties Billys hands behind him. Using the muzzle of the gun, they prod Billy in the direction they want him to go. Back at the training camp, they take Billy into the Princess's building. To inform her that they have captured a man who is probably responsible for the destruction of the armory.

The Princess turns to see who they've captured.

"You! I thought as much." She pulls her blaster and aims but doesn't fire.

"You two may leave us. I want to talk with your prisoner alone."

"There seems to be more to you than you let on Ace. You must be working for the Secret Police, especially since they turned up so fast at the castle to collect us."

"What makes you think I'm not working for myself, and just working with the Secret Police? Just so you know, my name is Billy Webber, just like my father."

"Now, why'd you do that?"

"Because the Sky Pirates killed my parents. Your brother killed my father, at least he confessed to it. Then your pirates killed my mother on the street not far from a bank they robbed. Now maybe you understand," says Billy with heat in his voice.

"Bad mistake that on my brother's part, and my mother's (Queen) part. I'm sorry that happened, but it did bring you to my attention."

"What's that to me?" asks Billy with contempt.

The Princess moves up close to Billy, touching his face with her hand, and then kisses him. "I find you fascinating; you're like no man I've ever met. You don't fawn over me or even make a pass at me, like the other men I've known. You did save me from Captain Rogers, on the Zeppelin. He was about to try to force his intentions upon my person."

"Look, Princess, I didn't come chasing out here to proclaim any undying love, I came to capture you and take you in."

"You don't like me even a Big?" said Vantessa in a pouty voice.

Billy doesn't answer her, but deep-down Billy finds her fascinating and dangerous, much like looking at a black widow spider. She's beautiful, but her bite is deadly. The Princess turns to the men, "we have to get out of here! He has called the Secret Police, and they'll be closing in."

An alarm is sounded, and everyone is assembled at the airfield. The Princess had found ten more men at the base and added them to her first six men. They all load onto the Zeppelin and fly out. For safekeeping, the Princess has Billy shackled and put into the brig aboard the Zeppelin.

"Men, if anyone hurts this man or he escapes, the people responsible will feel my wrath, and I can assure you it'll be very painful."

The Princess leaves the room to go to the bridge. She

knows of an island further North and not known to very many people. She hopes to pick up more recruits. Then to her final destination, which only she knows. In the brig, a huge man is watching over Billy. "What does the Princess see in you Big man?" criticizes the guard.

"She sees more in me than you do, my ugly friend," whispers Billy.

This gets the man riled up, he opens the door to the cell, picks Billy up by the front his shirt, and puts him face to face. "Now, Big man, what did you say about me?"

"I said you're ugly and very stupid," comments Billy.

"I'm going to break you in half, Big man!"

When they shackled Billy's feet, they left his hands free, and as the big man picks up Billy. Billy picks the man's pocket and lifted the keys to his cell and shackles.

"Hey ugly, before you do something you may regret, the Princess said to leave me alone, or she'd kill you," warns Billy.

The big man looks around and remembers what she did to him at the saloon on his island, and drops Billy onto the cell floor. "I'll kill you on another day, Big man!"

"Maybe, or I may kill you instead."

The big man gives a grunt, leaves the immediate area, and goes to the adjacent room. Billy takes out the keys and unlocks his shackles and the door to his cell. Billy looks around and finds a place to hide the key in case they capture him again. And they put him back in here. Billy finds a small space where the back of the cell bars meets the Zeppelins curved wall and manages to wedge the key into that cavity. Billy opens the cell door and goes to the only entrance to the brig, and cracks it open. He sees the big guy who so wants to kill him for calling him ugly and stupid. Billy opens the door and steps into the room as if he owns the place. The big guy jumps up and faces Billy.

"I'm going to kill you for this!" bellowed the big man.

The Big man charges at Billy like some big ape, and Billy stands there as if nothing is happening. Then Billy ducks under the big man's hands, and redirects his travel into the nearest rib of the Zeppelin. The man hit it so hard you could hear its sound almost to the other end of the ship. The man goes down in a heap. Billy checks him over, the force of hitting the rib broke his neck. Thinking to himself, *I didn't want to kill you.* Billy decides it'd be prudent to find a place to hide, so he heads toward the bowels of the ship, and tries to make his way to the cargo hold. Once in the cargo hold, Billy finds a place in some back corner, where he can move some of the large crates around and create a hiding spot to hold up.

News of Billy's escape soon reaches the Princess. "What! I told that big ape to stay away from the prisoner, and now he let him escape. Bring me that stupid man; I should've killed him the first time I saw him."

"Princess, the big guy as you call him is dead, his neck is broken."

"Good, it serves him right, throw the body overboard, and good riddance. Now I want every man jack of you to search this ship, and you'd better find him! That man is now more dangerous than you can imagine." screams the Princess.

The Princess calls down to the hangar area, get my plane ready. "I want it ready to fly just in case."

Billy manages to keep out of sight as they search for him, twice men sweep the cargo hold, Billy sits there hidden then realizes the Princess may have provided a way to escape. She'll have a plane in the hangar deck ready for her escape. Why not take advantage of it myself? Billy makes his way out of the cargo hold and heads down to the hangar deck, on the way he encounters one of the men, and before the man can pull his blaster, Billy puts him to sleep. Billy removes all the pirates' weapons. After dodging and hiding from a few more men, Billy makes his way to the hangar and finds the only plane. Its look's suspicious; there is no one guarding it. Billy sneaks his way to the aircraft and checks it over in one of the door panels next to the crystal engine; he sees an explosive device. Billy leaves the bomb intact, but removes it to the cockpit of the plane, and gets in. The door to launch bay is open.

"So, you'd try to kill me with a bomb, Princess." muses Billy.

Billy starts the plane and heads for the open door, as he passes the last section of the Zeppelin Billy pitches the bomb so when it goes off it'll not destroy the Zeppelin, but it'll disable it from flying very far, so he can track it down when the time comes.

The Princess watches as the plane leaves through the open bay door. "What it could've been Billy if you'd have agreed to be mine?" The Princess presses the button, and the plane doesn't explode, but the front of the Zeppelin is torn off, making it nearly impossible to steer.

"Billy! I'm going to kill you for this!" screams the Princess.

Billy flies off in a Southerly direction, and the Zeppelin

continues northward to a hidden island. Billy hopes that the transponder he planned on the Zeppelin in the cargo hold will keep working until he can come back with more Secret Police and put a final stop to the Sky Pirates.

The Princess manages to keep the Zeppelin in the air and still heading to the remote island. "That man is so exasperating! When I think I've outsmarted him and he always manages to come up with a way to escape me. I'm beginning to see that he's too dangerous to leave him alive."

Billy makes his way back to the training island. Billy lands the plane at the airstrip. Billy finds one of the more rundown hangars, and stashes the Secret Police plane inside, and covers it in broken debris to hide it. Thinking to himself, *one doesn't know when one will need a ready plane.* After he covers the plane, he hikes back to the South end of the island and uncovers his aircraft and flies it to the landing field next to the hangars. Billy hops out of his plane, then hears.

"Put up your hands!"

Billy complies with the request, and when he's turned around to face the huge man.

"Billy?"

"Bruiser?"

"It is you, Billy! Ok, men, you can come out now, it's Ok. I know this man."

Billy and Bruiser pound each other on the back, laughing together.

"Billy, it's so good to see you alive where's the Princess?"

"She got away, or rather I got away?"

"From you?" laughs Bruiser.

Chapter

16

Billy relates the story of getting here, then being captured by the Princess. Then his escape from the Zeppelin. The transponder he left on board the Zeppelin should make it easy for him to follow her.

"You guys sure got here fast; I wasn't expecting you for at least another day."

"The Captain sent us out after you the moment we lost your transponder, and it led us in this direction, and I remember the island it's where we were training to be Sky Pirates. So, we landed to scout it out, and that's when we found you."

"Bruiser, the good thing is that the Princess cannot travel very fast she blew up the front end of her Zeppelin to destroy me."

"She hates you that bad?"

"I don't think so; I think she may be in love with me because she keeps trying to win me over to her side. Besides, she could've killed me several times over and hasn't done it yet."

"If she loves you, I hate to see what she'd be like if she

hated you." Both men laugh.

"Me too, Bruiser."

"Billy, we need to get going if we are to capture the Princess."

"Ok, Bruiser, I'll lead in my plane. I'll turn on my transponder so you can follow me, and I'll be homing in on the transponder I left on the Princess's Zeppelin."

They shake hands, and Bruiser rounds up his men and hike back to their Zeppelin at the North end of the island. Billy sets up his transponder and turns it on. Then Billy flies off in the direction he was homed in on and heads toward the North. He hopes he can come within the range of the transponder Billy planted on Vantessa's Zeppelin so he can get a fix on Vantessa's position.

Once in the air, Bruiser outlines to the crew what's going to happen, that they're going to follow Billy's transponder signal, and he'll be following the Princess using the transponder he left on the Zeppelin, "so move out!" commands Bruiser.

Back on Vantessa's Zeppelin, the crew has a hard time keeping the Zeppelin in the air. As well as continuing on the flight path, the Princess has set course to return to her island. The pirates make temporary repairs. So, they limp along as best as they can. At this current rate of speed, *it'll take a few extra days, and that'll allow Billy and his dammed Secret Police to find them.* Thinks Vantessa.

Princess calls everyone to the bridge; with so few men at her disposal, they can almost fit into the small gondola.

"We have to fix this ship, or the Secret Police will catch up to us. Now, what are our options?" asks the Princess.

The men maul over the problem in their mind and what they know. Soon someone makes a suggestion.

"We could use the extra skin in stores and try to recover the opening, it'll take some time, but we could do it," says an aircraft mechanic.

"Ok, how long will it take?" demands the Princess.

"That depends your highness, on whether or not we can just float here to do the work or if we are going to keep moving."

"Ok, answer the question, if we float here or keep moving?" commands the Princess

"If we stay here for repairs one day if we keep moving, maybe three days."

"You have your day, and if you fail, realize that it's a long way down from where I will drop you off," said the Princess sternly.

"I understand your highness," said the mechanic.

The mechanic takes charge of the other men, and they rush to the store's locker to get the fabric to patch the large hole in the nose of the Zeppelin. They start at the top of the damage in the Zeppelin. Then, pull out the fabric with ropes and pulleys from the top of the Zeppelin to the bottom and then tie it in place so that the mechanic can have them start sewing the fabric in place by the end of the day as promised the Zeppelin is airworthy again. The Princess puts the ship back on course to her island. Then in her mind, she thinks of Billy; one side of her mind wants him dead. The other side of her mind admires him and considers him worthy of her love. *(That man is so exasperating!)* As the Princess mauls over Billy in her mind, she calls several men to the bridge. "That Policeman left a transponder on this ship, or he'd not have left. He'd have stayed on board to see where we were going, find that transponder, and find it now!" commands the Princess.

The crew take their leave of the Princess and head to the electronics room to get a couple of locators, and they start the search for the transponder. One group went to the forward end of the Zeppelin and one group to the aft end, and the last group went high up to the Zeppelin structure, and they all turned on the locators, they find the frequency and triangulate to the transponder's location. The men converge on the place in the cargo hold to search for the transponder, and they find the hiding place where Billy had placed the transponder. One of her men turns it off.

The man in charge reports to the Princess that they've turned off the transponder and hands it to her. The Princess turns it over in her hands as she looks it over.

"Very good; you didn't destroy it; I can use this to lure Billy back to me. So, I can capture him and his Secret Police. Here go put this away for now." The Princess hands the transponder back to the crewman.

"Very well, highness." The crewman turns away and leaves with the transponder.

Billy figures the Princess will locate his transponder soon enough, but he has her heading and will stay with that in hopes that he'll find her. Billy flies off in the direction of his latest readings, and he can still pick up the transponder. Billy gets a fix on her position, then the transponder signal quits. Billy calls the Secret Police, following him to continue to follow him. He tells them that the Princess has found the transponder and has turned it off. Billy has her heading and will continue flying in that direction for the time being.

The Princess calls her men to her so that she can outline her plans, so when they land at the hidden base, there will be no error or mistakes. The base already has a small contingent of Sky Pirates and supplies. "We'll land and make sure of the repairs to the ship, and load on all the supplies then we'll desert the base. We're taking everyone with us. We'll head back to the castle where my mother ruled. I want to pick up some money so we can restock and buy more men."

The men break up and return to their stations to await the landing. The next morning, they land, and the men set out to follow the Princess's orders, they contact the pirates in residence and get them to help load the supplies. The repairs to the Zeppelin take a few days. Then the Princess takes the transponder and turns it on for Billy to find with a note. (*Sorry to have missed you. Better luck next time. Next time I intend to kill you! signed Vantessa.*) The Princess and crew set off for the island with the castle so that the Princess can raid the treasure vault. The trip to the castle will take at least a week.

As Billy flies along, the tracker starts to sound off that the transponder has been reactivated. Billy thinks to himself, *what are you planning, Princess? It'll either be a taunt or a trap. I wonder what it'll be.* Billy continues to fly in the direction the transponder was leading him. Billy calls to the Zeppelin that's following him and reports that his transponder he left with the Princess is on. Billy warns them of a trap. Billy soon finds the island and circles his plane looking for the Zeppelin, and when he doesn't spot it, he lands his plane and gets out to check the airfield. Billy looks into the buildings with his blaster drawn but soon discovers the place is abandoned. Then he spots his transponder and the note the Princess left him.

Speaking to himself, *"Well, Princess, I see that it's a taunt, where'd you go? And when did you leave here?"* thinks Billy.

Billy takes the time to look around through all the buildings. Billy soon finds what looks like an office, and he reads the papers and files. Then Billy comes upon a map of the world Topaz and sees what islands are marked on it. Billy locates the castle island and then the training island; he then locates the island he is on now. As Billy studies the map, he sees other places the pirates have marked on the map showing hidden bases.

The Secret Police will be able to raid all these places and put an end to the Sky Pirates.

As Billys studies the map of Topaz the Secret Police Zeppelin following him catches up to him and lands. Seeing the light on in the one building, they all converge there to find Billy sitting behind a desk with his feet up.

"Well, Captain, I think I've found something of great value. Here's a map showing all the locations where the Sky Pirates have bases; we can now put them out of commission."

"Billy, you're a wonder, I wonder why she didn't destroy this place and any evidence that may be here?"

"Could be a couple of reasons Captain, when I was a Sky

Pirate there was a conspiracy within the ranks, no one except the leader here even knew this existed. I believe we're fortunate to find it," stated Billy.

"Do you know where she went, Billy?" asks the Captain.

"Not yet, Captain, I need to think about it. I know she needs money to pay her men, that means a robbery, or she may have a hidden stash. As I recall, the Secret Police have not yet recovered any of the stolen jewels, or money to date." muses Billy.

"Where do you think she'd go? To one of these islands?" as he points to the map.

"Remembering her mother, the Queen, she trusted no one, not even her family, so she'd want the money and treasure close to hand, and readily available. In case of need. My guess would be she is going to the castle," said Billy.

"We have that place occupied. The Princess can't land, especially a Zeppelin."

"Captain, that may not mean much, there're other nearby islands, we may need to have them all searched and a man stationed there to keep watch," said Billy.

"Bruiser, come here!" orders the Captain.

"Yes, sir!" snapping to attention and saluting.

"I want you to organize the men to stake out these Islands, give them blasters, and radios. If they encounter the pirate's Zeppelin, they're to call it in on the double. Then clear the area," ordered the Captain.

"Yes, Sir, may I ask how, sir?" queries Bruiser.

"Just offload the planes in the lower hangar, between the planes and men you should have enough to cover the nearby islands where the castle is," commands the Captain.

"Yes sir!" and Bruiser salutes the Captain and turns to execute the order.

Bruiser directs the hangar crew to offload the planes and to make sure the aircraft are ready to fly. Bruiser assembles his men and gives them their orders. "Now jump to it, you bunch of gold bricks!" shouts Bruiser. The men run to the armory and then to their planes, and soon they have offloaded the planes from off the Zeppelin; then, they soon takeoff heading to their assigned islands.

Billy walks up to Bruiser and tells him he's heading for the castle island to wait for the Princess to show up so he can capture her.

"I know what trouble you can get into, so I'll go with you," said Bruiser.

Billy punches Bruiser in the shoulder good-naturedly, and says, "Let's get going."

They take Bruiser's plane that has two seats, Billy sits in the co-pilot seat, and Bruiser pilots the plane. On their way to the island, Billy tells Bruiser all that has happened since they parted. Billy asks Bruiser to tell his friend Jim if something happens to him. Bruiser promises to go to his childhood friend and guardian and tell him all that has transpired. laughs Bruiser.

Chapter

17

"Well, children, it's time to go make lunch, and then we can get back to the story."

"Ahh! Grandpa, do we have to it's getting exciting, can't we keep going?"

Mom and Dad speak up now; children go wash up for lunch, and then grandpa can get back to his story."

"Alright, mom."

Both kids run off to wash up. Then mom and dad go into the house with grandpa to make lunch.

"Dad your story is great, you're keeping us enthralled the whole time with your narration, I'm so glad I'm recording this."

"Thank you, son; I wasn't sure I was going to be up to the task of telling Billy's story. You and the children are making me glad I'm doing this. Well, let's get lunch together."

After the meal, grandpa gets a tall glass of ice-cold cider.

"Now that hits the spot. Well, son; are you ready for me to continue my story?"

"There, Dad, any time you're ready. The recorder is warmed up and ready to go."

Grandpa gets back into the story of Billy Webber and the Sky Pirates. After ten minutes of talking, grandpa has everyone on the edge of their seat, hanging on his every word.

Billy and Bruiser get to the island with the Sky Pirates castle, Billy leaves Bruiser to contact the other Secret Police to be on guard, the Princess will be coming here soon. Billy enters the castle and goes to the Queen's quarters in the castle to search her rooms; he's unsure what he's looking for. He moves every tapestry, and piece of furniture. Billy is looking for anything out of place. He tests the walls looking for hidden switches, doors, and such hoping he manages to locate where the Queen stashed her treasure.

Billy spends hours looking, and he even has some of the men help him. They don't seem to find anything until one of the men asks Billy.

"Sir, why is this pipe here? It doesn't seem to be connected to anything or serve any real function."

"How big is that pipe officer?" queries Billy.

"Come and see, it looks to be about a foot in diameter, and the lid pops right up."

"Interesting," said Billy. "Does anyone have a torchlight?"

"I do, Sir." The Policeman extends it toward Billy.

"Let me have it." The Policeman passes his touch to Billy, and he shines it into the pipe, and it's so deep the light cannot see the bottom. Billy drops the torchlight and watches it as it falls. After a short time, the torchlight goes out, but the sound it makes when it hits bottom seems wrong.

"I have it!" said Billy "this is where the Queen has been dropping the loot, and it has been collecting down under the castle. You men see if you can trace this pipe down under the castle. Bruiser, we need a boat."

In an hour, Bruiser and Billy are motoring around the island. Seeking for a cave entrance on the backside of the castle at the water level. They don't see it, because the tide is in and it's covered. Billy and Bruiser don't know that there is a cave entrance. They pass by and circle the whole island for several hours.

"Bruiser, it has to be there. There has to be a way into the treasure chamber!"

"Billy, it's probably right in front of us, and we don't see it yet."

"Bruiser, what'd you just say?"

"It's in front of us; we don't see it yet."

"Yes, that's it, the tide, when the tide goes out, you can see it. Any word on the Zeppelin?"

"No one has called in about it. But there's one lookout they've not reached for a while."

"Has anyone been sent to see if he's still living? I'd not be surprised to find the Princess is there," said Billy.

Bruiser grabs his radio and calls into command. "Any word from the man on the nearby island who has not called in yet?"

"No, Sir, he has not called in for hours. Did you want me to send someone?"

"You haven't sent back up to look into this problem, why

not?"

"Sorry, sir."

"Jump to it, cadet, find out why he is not answering!"

"Yes, sir, right away, Sir!"

"Well, Billy, what do we do now? Go to the island or look for the entrance to the treasure?"

"Let's look for the treasure Bruiser; the Princess will come to us, once we find it."

Billy and Bruiser head back to the dock and wait for the tide to go out. At high tide, Billy and Bruiser motor out to the backside of the castle to sit and wait for the tide to go out. To see what may be hidden in the cliff rocks below the castle.

Chapter

18

The Princess had anticipated Billy looking for the treasure, and so she landed her Zeppelin at the nearby island a day before Billy and Bruiser had even gotten to the castle island. She did not trust her men with the location of the cave entrance. The Princess went alone in a motorboat. At low tide, she enters the cave and loads up her boat with some gold bars and many jewels. The gold would be too heavy to move and would swamp the boat; the jewels are lighter in weight, so she took as many as she could find Vantessa loaded so many gems she could buy a kingdom of her own. This'd keep her, and her men supplied for a long time.

The Princess figures that Billy will soon find the cave and have all the money removed, so this had to be a onetime withdrawal. The jewels are worth more by weight than the gold or silver bars. With her boat loaded, she just gets out of the cave before the tide closed the cave entrance. She makes it back to the island where her men were waiting for her.

"Men load this on to the Zeppelin, put it into the brig, and put guards on it. If so, much as one bauble is missing, I'll kill the guards and the person who stole anything. Is this clear!"

"Yes Princess."

The helmsman asks "Princess, where are we going?"

"We're headed to the biggest island, and we'll come at it from the East side."

"But Princess, we're on the West side of the island already."

"You know that, and I know that, so does the Secret Police. They'll be looking for us in the remote parts of Topaz. In the meantime, we'll become respectable merchants. We'll pick up some cargo as we fly along to sell at the main port. We'll be able to mix in with the other Zeppelins, sell our cargo, and then buy us some planes and supplies."

"We'll hide in plain sight?" asks the crewman.

"You got it. Now get the Zeppelin loaded, and let's get out of here," commands the Princess.

During loading, the Secret Policeman is dropped off to survey that very island. Before he can go more than a mile, he's intercepted by the pirates and killed.

"Sir, this is guard post one, a Secret Policeman has landed, and I've killed him."

"Alright guard post one return to the Zeppelin, I'll pass on the information to the Princess."

"Yes, Sir."

"Princess, this is guard command, the Secret Police have landed a man on the island, and he's been eliminated."

"How long-ago command?"

"Just moments ago, Princess."

"Get everyone on board now! We need to leave!"

"Yes, Princess."

An hour later, the Zeppelin lifts off and starts their journey around the world to collect cargo and some men. Vantessa promotes a few men. She gathers the department heads and shows them the treasure she has gathered so that they can tell the men. Then she and the department heads start planning what cargo to pick up and what they'll do to get the planes and supplies they'll need for the future. She also is looking for a new island base, to reestablish the Sky Pirate base.

Back at the castle island, a few hours later, the tide goes out, and Bruiser spots the cave entrance as the tide moves out. Billy and Bruiser wait until they can enter the cave. They motor into the cave entrance and follow it back until they see the treasure scattered all over the floor, gold, silver, and jewels. The preverbal king's fortune.

"We'll take several days to remove all this treasure the Sky Pirates have amassed here," said Bruiser.

"I wonder if the Princess has been here already or not?" ponders Billy aloud.

"Who knows?" said Bruiser.

They take a Big time to wander through the treasure chamber, and as they are about to leave, Billy spots a white envelope placed on a ledge. Billy walks over to pick it up and sees his name on it. Billy opens the letter and begins to read.

"Dear Billy, with this letter, you can assume that I've been here and picked up some of the treasure. I knew you'd figure out where it was, and try to stop me. Well-beloved, I've outsmarted you again.

I hope to continue this game of chase. After all, a girl likes to be chased after. I wonder if you can figure my next move. I look forward to running into you again. Love and kisses. The Princess of the Sky Pirates. PS I intend to kill you at our next meeting."

"Some love letter Billy."

"The problem is Bruiser is she means every word of it."

"Say it isn't so Billy, you like her, don't you!"

"Yes, I have to admit it, Bruiser, I do like her. I don't know why. It's probably the danger aspect of her."

"Billy, she threatens to kill you."

"The Princess could've killed me a few times over Bruiser and didn't do it. She even kissed me, and it was a thrill then. I'll catch up to her, it's just a matter of time. We had best leave, or we'll be stuck here until morning."

Billy and Bruiser leave the cave and head back to the dock, Billy gets with the Commander in charge and tells him what he has discovered and that they need to collect the treasure beneath the castle. With that done, Billy and Bruiser call the Captain, to have the men recalled. Billy has to explain that the Princess has money now and needs to come up with a new plan to track down the Princess and the Sky Pirates.

"Well, Billy, you've done the best job of following her to date, just continue."

"Yes, Captain, I'll do the best I can. I need to work with Bruiser on this, sir."

"Use whoever you need, Billy, but bring her in. I want the Sky Pirates to stop!"

Billy and Bruiser salute the Captain and walk away.

"The Captain sure served up a tall order for you, Billy,

what're we going to do?" asks Bruiser.

"Right now, try to figure out what she is going to do, then try to get there first," muses Billy.

"Billy, what would you do in her place?"

"The Princess needs to convert the jewels into cash, and she can only do that in a few cities where she can get a fair deal on them," said Billy.

"Which cities, Billy?"

"She'll have to disguise her Zeppelin to look like a cargo ship, and not a military one. Then she must land at a port, where she can restock and recruit more men."

"What about the largest city on the large continent?" queried Bruiser.

"Bruiser, that's what I'd do in her place. Go someplace where she'd not stand out. A place where she can resupply and maybe get arms and planes. Let's go; we'll take my plane. It's faster than the ones the Secret Police use," said Billy.

"We'd better get some supplies ourselves; it's a long flight to Mid-city," comments Bruiser.

"Ok Bruiser, you take care of it; I'm going to check out the plane. Meet me at the airfield with the supplies."

An hour later, Bruiser shows up at Billy's plane to load the supplies on board.

"Billy, how do we find the Princess when we get to Mid-city?"

"I'm not sure Bruiser, but I've been lucky so far. I hope to run on to the Princess quickly; we'll have to haunt some of the places where she may show up."

"Can you narrow that down a bit, Mid-city is a huge place," complains Bruiser.

"I figure she's going to fence the jewels, and she is going to want top dollar for them; we can find and stake out the shop where she might head. Also, she is going to want planes to carry out her robberies."

"Billy, how are we going to stake out all the places so we can find her?" asks Bruiser.

"The Captain is calling ahead to have a small group of men waiting for us, so we'll be able to cover more ground," states Billy.

"That's nice to know. The two of us would get spread pretty thin in a hurry."

"You worry too much, Bruiser, we'll find her, and stop her. Finish loading the supplies, and I'll be back; I want to lay some misdirection in case we still have a mole in our midst."

Chapter
19

Bruiser loads up the supplies, and while that's happening, Billy goes to the radio shack to send a message to Head Quarters (HQ) to let them know that he and Bruiser are heading out to circumnavigate the globe to look for the Princess. Billy returns to the plane and finishes checking out the rest of the aircraft. Then both men get in and make ready for takeoff. Once in the air, Billy heads out in the direction he indicated per his radio call. Then drops down to near sea level and turns to head for Mid-city directly. As Billy suspected, a coded message is sent to the Princess, telling her that Billy is following her.

The Princess continues on her course for Mid-city by circumnavigating the world to approach from the east. Billy will approach Mid-city from the West, and reach there a few days before the Princess. Billy takes his plane to his old stomping grounds and lands at the airport where he grew up and parks his plane in the hangar.

"Billy, why're we here?"

"I wanted to land and park where we'd not be easily found; this is my old hangar. No one will look for us here. We can catch the bus to Mid-city from here and arrive unannounced and without leaving a record."

"Sounds good to me," said Bruiser. "What do we do now?"

"Follow me." Billy leads Bruiser into his hangar. Billy opens a door into what looks like an office, and he points to a bed. "You sleep there, and I'll sleep upstairs."

"Oh, good, it's been a good long three days getting here, and I'm beat." Bruiser falls into his bed and is soon fast asleep.

Billy, too is not long in falling asleep in his bed; the next morning, his friend Jim is shaking him awake.

"Huh, what?" asks Billy.

"Hey, your back," said Jim.

"It's just a stopover Jim; we're on our way to Mid-city to catch a pirate."

"I can help if you like, you can borrow my car."

"No, Jim! You need to get away from me and stay away. I don't want you anywhere near this, or it could get you and your family into harm's way. Ok!"

"Alright, Billy, but it's nice seeing you." Jim gets up, and leaves Billy's hangar, and returns to his own.

"Billy, is that the Jim you want me to talk to and tell your story to if you don't get back from this?"

"The very one."

"He seems to be a good guy; I like him."

"He tried to adopt me when my mother was killed, but his wife protested. So, I ran away and moved in here. He found me and left me to myself, but he always looked after me.

Taught me to work on planes, and then helped me build one of my own. He even got the best pilot instructor to teach me how to fly."

"Wow, I do want to get to know him," said Bruiser.

"Let's shake a leg Bruiser; we need to clean up and change out of these clothes into some civvies."

Both change their clothes and look much like the common people around them, so they don't draw any attention.

"Here we'll meet with the men that the Captain sent for us at the pub near the Zeppelin docking port, they'll be looking for us to be there at noon, so let's shake a leg and get moving," said Billy.

They arrive at the pub on time. They belly up to the bar and order a round of drinks. Then Billy and Bruiser move off to an empty table off to the side of the room to wait for the men to show up. Five men enter the pub, look around the room, and spot Billy and Bruiser over to the side by themselves. They walk up to the bar, buy some drinks, and meander over to Billy's table.

"Would you mind if we joined you, sir?"

"Sure, sit down, there is plenty of room," says Billy.

The men sat and started chatting over everyday things, like women, weather, and such. When Billy sees that, the crowd is well away from their table.

"Who sent you? Queried Billy."

One of the men looked around, and said the "Captain sent us."

"You know why we're here and what you're to do?" challenged Billy.

"No, sir, we don't know, he said you'd fill us in, and that we're to follow your orders."

"Very good then." Billy points to the men, you two cover the Zeppelin docking ports see who comes in, and look for any Zeppelins that look like they were recently painted. Barring that, keep a weather eye out for a Zeppelin that looks old with no markings. Report to me as soon as possible. Here is my address, leave a message with the clerk," commands Billy.

"What'd you want the rest of us to do, sir?" asks one of the other men.

"I want you and Bruiser here to go to the Plane manufactures and see if anyone has or will be placing a large order for ten planes or more."

Billy shakes Bruiser's hand as he and the young lad leave to check out their part.

Billy turns to the last man, "you're with me; we'll be checking out, possible places where jewelry and gold can be sold." They get up and start for town. The first two go to the Zeppelin port and ask the port master if any Zeppelins have arrived today and where they're docked. The men go and check out the new arrivals and find nothing like what Billy suggests. So, they pick out a place to sit and watch.

Bruiser and his partner canvas, the airplane manufacturers. Looking to see if anyone has recently purchased any new planes. Again, they strike out and realize that the Princess hasn't yet shown up, or the Princess has gone somewhere else. Billy and his partner find a similar situation. Billy thinks that's a good thing. That means that they may have gotten here ahead of the Princess, now all they have to do is wait for her to arrive. That night at Billy's and Bruiser's room, all the men meet and confess they've not found anything about the Princess. Billy explains it's a good thing in that she hasn't yet arrived, and so now we're ahead of her, and she can now fly into our trap. They break up for the night and return to their rooms to wait for the morning. The next day Billy deploys his men to the Zeppelin port to watch for incoming cargo ships. Billy stays behind and comes up with a disguise for him and Bruiser. He makes them look older and with beards and glasses. Then they hobble to the port to check on the men. Billy hobbles up to one of the men and asks if he can have some change for a drink, and to Billy's surprise, the young man gives it to him.

Bruiser does the same thing to the man he was with yesterday and gets the same response. These guys would let the Princess walk right by them even if she did show up. Billy admonishes the men for being careless. A week goes by with no result. Billy is beginning to suspect *the Princess may have gone to another port city. To cash in her jewels, and order her planes from there, but which one?* In the meantime, one of the men informs Billy of an airplane order of twenty, so Billy and the man rush to the aircraft company only to find that the military ordered them.

The Princess had her Zeppelin make several stops along the way so she could purchase supplies and some cargo so the Zeppelin would appear no different than any of the other cargo ships. When she reaches Mid-city docking facilities and offloads the cargo, they should go unnoticed. The

Princess plans to stay on board ship and let her men do all the transactions. She figures that Billy will be there looking for her, let's don't tip our hand just yet. She has a couple of the men set up to purchase a couple of planes from each of the aircraft companies, so as not to present any red flags that might catch Billy's attention. The Princess has used the time well on her trip around the world. She plans to make sure she can escape with her ship and men. The Princess plans on the last day to show herself just before takeoff so that Billy will continue to follow her.

After the second week, Billy is ready to give up and start searching for the Princess in another city when her Zeppelin docks at the Mid-city port. It has a new paint job, but most of all, the damage to the front of the Zeppelin still shows the repairs.

"Bruiser, go bring the men here, I'll continue to watch this Zeppelin to see what's going on."

"Are you sure, Billy? Remember, she wants to kill you, you know."

"I don't think they'll notice me in my disguise; Bruiser now get going," commands Billy.

Bruiser dashes off to gather the men to where Billy is, for more orders about what Billy will have them doing.

The Princess uses the telescope. She was looking down onto the dockyard below. To see if anything is going on when she spots Billy in his disguise.

"So, you're on to me, are you, my love. Well, I'll give you a nice reception. You'll not stop my plans this time." The Princess purrs.

Billy doesn't know that he's been made, so he chooses to linger about the Zeppelin docking port, hoping that he can capture the Princess. The Princess calls a couple of her men and shows them, Billy, down on the dock. She instructs them to capture him alive and unhurt; they're to use a sleep dart to subdue him and bring him here and put him into the brig in chains.

Two men dispatched by the Princess dress down to what the other workers are wearing down on the dock and walk right up to Billy from behind. Before Billy realizes he's in danger, he's put to sleep with a dart that's stabbed into his arm. The man that was his partner is not so fortunate; the other man stabs him in the back right through his heart, killing him. As Billy slumps over, the man who used the dart holds him up, and his friend grabs Billy's other free arm, stumbling down the dock as if drunk. They lurch and stumble about back to the ship. Then a commotion occurs when someone finds the dead body with a knife wound in his back. This makes the three men even more un-noticed as they return to the Zeppelin. Once they have Billy in the brig, they put chains on him and remove his disguise, then they lock him in and place a guard on him.

That night Bruiser and the men meet, and he gets concerned when Billy and his partner don't turn up. Just as Bruiser gets up to find Billy, Bruiser hears a knock at the door. Bruiser opens it to see a policeman standing there. He delivers the news that one of Bruiser's people is at the morgue dead. Bruiser asks, "is Billy with him?" The response is no.

Thanks, said Bruiser, the policeman leaves. Bruiser turns

to the men to get suggestions as to what they need to do to find Billy. One of the men suggests, why not dress up as secret police and raid the last two Zeppelins that came to port. Then inspect it from top to bottom.

"Alright, I like doing things direct, so let's do it, and we'll have to move fast, which Zeppelin was last in port?"

"Billy said the Zeppelin with the damaged front end, that had been repaired that'll be the Princess's ship."

"Good, we'll hit that one first. Man-up and meet me at the dock in thirty minutes."

"Yes, Sir!"

Thirty minutes later, they meet in the lobby in uniform; they leave to go to the docks. Soon after the Princess captures Billy and puts him into the brig, the Princess offloads a few of her men to take the jewels to a broker and then go purchase supplies and the planes they're to meet her at the airfield outside of Mid-city. Once the men were departed with the cargo of jewels, she sets sail, telling the authorities that she is behind schedule for the next cargo drop. By the time Bruiser and his men reached the port, he sees them off in the distance as the Zeppelin sails away.

"Hurry men, we have to get to the base and requisition some fast planes to follow them," said Bruiser.

The men dash to the street and look for a taxi to take them to the Secret Police base. The Princess's Zeppelin has taken flight and sails up into the clouds then heads for the airport outside of the city. She does not land; she knows it'll take a couple of days for the men to exchange the jewels for usable cash, and purchase the planes for delivery. Bruiser and his men make it to the base, and with all the red tape, he's slowed down from acquiring the planes he needs. Two days later they get the requested planes, but by this time, the Princess could be anywhere. Bruiser realizes they lost Billy to the Princess's clutches, and she'll kill him before long. Bruiser begins to think, *"What would Billy do?"*

Chapter

20

In the brig, Billy wakes up chained to the cell wall, he starts looking around for a way to get loose, when he hears footsteps coming from around the corner, sounds like a man and a woman with a type of high heel, as they clanked on the wood deck.

"Billy, my love, are you comfortable? I hope not too much!" purrs the Princess.

"I'm comfortable now that you're here, I assume we're underway. I can fell the vibrations of the motors through the deck," answers Billy.

"How perceptive of you to notice. Now, tell me what the Secret Police are up to."

"They're trying to catch up to you and put you in prison," comments Billy.

"I know that much, Billy dear, what I want to know is how they plan to do that? Where are they? What places should I avoid?"

"I can tell you this much, Princess; I don't know what the

Secret Police are up to. The people in charge don't tell me much. I'm a bit low on that food chain." answers Billy.

"Oh, you're not going to tell me, is that it?" purrs the Princess.

Vantessa opens the door to the cell and places a hand on his shoulder next to his neck and applies a pinch, expecting Billy to writhe in pain. Billy sits there and looks up at her and smiles. The Princess slaps his face then stands back from Billy.

"You've had the training in the fighting arts!" asks the angry Princess.

"Yes, I have." laughs Billy.

The Princess hits Billy on his chest with both hands in frustration. "I hate you!" she screams. Then he turns and walks away. The Princess leaves a guard to watch Billy after she leaves the brig and closes the cell door.

The Princess turns to the guard "I'll send another guard to relieve you, don't open this door until he arrives. Do you understand?!"

"Yes, Princess."

The Princess walks off, muttering to herself.

"I think she's a bit upset with me; don't you think?" asks Billy.

The guard at the door says nothing but stands at attention.

"I see; it's smart not to talk to the prisoner, you might go far in her organization. When your friend arrives, could you lose me so I can use the can in the corner?" asks Billy.

The guard says nothing. Billy sits in the quiet and watches the activity outside his cell and begins to think of a way to get away so he can stop the Princess before she can start her reign of terror that the Sky Pirates had brought by her mother, the Queen. A short time later, the second guard arrives.

"Guys, may I be allowed to use the bucket in the corner, please!" pleads Billy.

The two men talked together for a moment, then one of them drew his blaster and moves to one side. So, his partner doesn't block his shot as he opens the cell to unlock Billy from his chains so he can use the bathroom. Billy seeing that the outside guard covers him, decides not to jump the man in his cell; he uses the can and sits back down on his seat to be chained up. Then the guard locks the cell door. Billy figures if he doesn't put up a fight just yet, he may catch his guards off guard the next time.

Later that day, the Princess has Billy brought to her private room, where she has dinner set up for them. The guards are still present, and they have their guns in their hands. Billy looks over his shoulder and sees them.

"Are you that afraid of me, Princess?" questions Billy.

"No, not of you, I just don't trust you."

"I guess I can live with that; do you have someplace where I can wash up for dinner?" asks Billy.

"The washbasin is over there." Points the Princess with a wave of her hand. Billy takes off his shirt and soaps his hand and face, then he dries off and puts his shirt back on.

"Now, what're we having for dinner?" asks Billy.

"It'll be here shortly, I had it specially prepared for us." states the Princess.

"I see, if it's like your mother served at the last banquet, this should be good."

"Now, tell me what the Secret Police have in mind for capturing me." the Princess purrs.

"At the moment I don't know, the plans changed once you captured me. I was to capture you and bring you in. Now, as you can see, that failed." laments Billy.

"Now my love, give me your word you'll do nothing to escape or cause any trouble, and I'll send the guards out of here."

"I'll give you my word, not to escape, or cause any trouble for now," said Billy.

The Princess points to the guards, "wait outside of the door; only let the server come into the room with the food."

The guards obey, and shortly after that, the server pushed in a cart full of food. Billy used all of his etiquettes at dinner. To impress the Princess, with any hope of putting her at ease. At first not much is said, then Billy asks the Princess about her family. She looks up at the ceiling then she looks at Billy to see if he is mocking her. Vantessa sees that he's not mocking her, but is genuinely interested. Then she looks at the table in front of her.

"Ok, I'll tell you about my family, if you'll tell me about your family."

"That seems fair. You go first," said Billy.

The Princess takes a deep breath, more to collect her thoughts. Then she launches into her story.

"My grandfather owned property in the interior of the largest island, and on it, he found a large cache of energy crystals. He took samples to the office of energy; they classified it as top grade and offered to pay top dollar for the lot that he had. Grandfather sold the crystals and bought equipment to start mining the crystal. My grandfather saw the climate change politically, so he took the precaution to transport the mined crystal to a safe hiding place, then sold more crystal to the authorities. One morning, the military moves in and evicts my grandad and his family and takes over the mine.

My grandfather gathers his mine workers and trains them to fight, and they learn how to fly. Using the crystals, he had stashed away. Then he starts raiding the mine as they brought up big shipments of the crystal. When that got to be too dangerous, my grandfather moves on to banks. He bought an island where he builds a castle. On one raid, he is killed, and my mother takes over, you remember her Billy."

"I do remember her. But you don't need to be like her, turn yourself in and disband the Sky Pirates. I'll stand by you, and do all that I can to help you with your trial. When you get out of prison, I'll be there for you." states Billy.

The Princes laugh, "Right, like they gave my grandfather that choice. Don't you understand they want my family and me dead, so they have no one to lay claim to the crystal mine? You see Billy, my family still owns that property, and the corrupt officials (The Five) are lining their pockets with money that belongs to me." said the Princess.

"I'll check into that too. You have my word," states Billy.

"Now that I've shown you my past such as it is, what about yours?"

Chapter

21

"Fair enough, my father was killed in the line of duty spying on the Sky Pirates; he's the one who saved your brother. Then he was shot down, and his plane exploded, killing him. When I was eighteen years old, the Sky Pirates killed my mother so that they could get away from the police after robbing a bank. They open fire on the people in the street to create a diversion; my mother was killed, leaving me without any parents. Now you know why I want to take down the Sky Pirates," said Billy with some heat.

"That's not true; they don't kill innocent people." screams the Princess.

"Tell that to a eighteen-year-old boy, who went to his mother's funeral. May I be excused and returned to my cell?" demands Billy.

"Guards, return the prisoner to his cell." After the door closed, the Princess is heartbroken, and she runs off to her room to cry; in her heart, she knows Billy is right in what he told her. She is heartless in her dealings with people in general, but she lost her heart to that eighteen-year-old boy, now a man.

Bruiser is chomping at the bit to go after Billy and save him, but the red tape seems to get in the way. That night Bruiser and the men assigned to help Billy leave the base and head to the airfield where they steal three planes. The plan is to fly off and search the close-by airfields from the air in hopes of locating the Sky Pirate's Zeppelin. They know the purchase of the planes that happened a day ago was for the Princess, and Bruiser knows that they'll need to catch up to the Zeppelin to load them on board, not to mention the supplies.

Later that night, the Princess comes to Billy's cell. "Beloved, get up."

"What is it Princess, are you going to kill me now too!?"

"No, I'm going to let you go, my family has done far too much to your family, (Her voice almost breaks) I want you to leave this ship and don't follow me. The next time I'll have to kill you, and the thought of it breaks my heart. Please go and don't ever find me again." The Princess pleads.

The Princess and the guards take Billy down to the hangar deck, and they give Billy a gravity pack, which will let him descend to the ground in safety. Billy puts on the pack and weighs his chances of survival if he took on the men then captures the Princess. Then Billy turns and jumps out the chute, and descends to the ground. Billy just realized she is a bit kinder to him than usual, he had to admit that he had fallen for the Princess himself, but he cannot let that get in his way of capturing her.

As Billy descends to the ground, he hears the Zeppelin's motors fire up, and he looks up to see the Zeppelin ascend into the clouds above to a height where he can no longer see it. As the Zeppelin disappears into the cloud cover above, they continued in the direction that they were traveling, and Billy notes it until everything goes silent. Billy strained his ears to listen for the Zeppelin, but when he lands on the ground, he cannot say for sure where it's headed, Eastward or Westward from his position, because it went silent.

The Princess has the Zeppelin go quiet and continues to gain altitude. At ten thousand feet, she fires up the motors and does a slow turn back to the port they had left. Thinking that Billy and the Secret Police wouldn't believe Vantessa would return. They'll think she'll use the time to run away and put some distance between her and the police. Billy makes his landing and runs to the watchtower to only find he has landed at the airport where he used to live; he locates a phone to call the base and let them know he's safe and that the Princess got away. Billy decides to wait for the police to come and pick him up. Knowing it'll be a few hours before anyone arrives, Billy decides to go to his hangar and crash. He's exhausted, and he has some thinking to do. Did the Government cause the Sky Pirates to come into being? Billy decides to suspend finding the Princess for now and turn over a new rock she had given him.

Several hours later, Bruiser is shaking Billy awake. "Billy, how'd you get away?" insisted Bruiser.

"I could spin you a very daring yarn, but in all reality, she let me go. After our dinner, she gave me a landing pack and dropped me off here."

"Does she know where you live, Billy?"

"I don't think so; I think this is just a coincidence. At dinner, the Princess and I had a discussion. And I found out that our Government may be responsible for the Sky Pirates, and I'm going to find out."

"Billy, are you sure that's a wise thing to do?" question Bruiser.

"No Bruiser, I don't, but it'll explain some things that I've encountered since working for the Secret Police. They're as corrupt as the Government or as the Sky Pirates. Something to think about?"

"Are you ready for a ride back to base? We can stay here for a while if you need to?" said Bruiser.

"Let's go, Bruiser, then I'm going to the hall of records, to check out and see if what the Princess told me is true. Then I'll approach the Captain with the evidence to see what he'll do", answers Billy.

"I think you'd better keep your plane ready Billy, if this goes bad, you may need it."

"I hear you, Bruiser."

Bruiser returns them to base, and when they arrive, Billy reports in to be debriefed about his time with the Princess. Billy doesn't tell them what he has been notified. He keeps it to himself. Afterward, he gets permission to go to the hall of records to investigate a hunch. The Captain gives him leave to do so. Billy goes the hangar and checks out his plane then flies off to Mid-city on the far side of the island. When Billy arrives, he goes to the central file's office; it's open for the day. Billy shows the paper of permissions Billy received from the Captain to review the restricted records section. Billy opens a file drawer showing what lands were confiscated, and he locates a record for the crystal mine on the island. It was condemned deemed unsafe to be worked. Then Billy finds files of how much crystal the Government mined out of that crystal mine, but no money is disclosed. Billy looks up the people who were responsible for the land grab and discovers that their money accounts skyrocketed, and they're now wealthy beyond imagination.

"I got you now, and I see the Princess was right and did not lie to me. Now to take this to the Captain to see what he does." Thinks Billy on his way to see the Captain, Billy makes copies of all the documents and hides them for the future. Billy also engages a way to stash more copies of the materials in a safe place if something should happen to him.

Chapter

22

"Ok, I've babbled on long enough, you guys. I'm hungry and thirsty, and there is still a lot more story to be told. We all need a break."

"Grandpa, it was getting good," complains Jeff.

"Jeff, you were glued to the floor, so I guess it must be good, but I need substance, food, and the like."

"I hear you, dad!" said Colleen.

Colleen rounds up everyone and heads them into the kitchen to rustle up some grub for everyone. Grandpa and Doug head for the root cellar to locate some cider, where Grandpa pulls out some hard cider and gives Doug a cup of it then takes a bit for himself. Grandpa watches Doug take a drink and laughs when Doug nearly chocks on it. "Oh, that has quite a kick." gasps Doug.

Grandfather tosses down his drink and wipes his lips on his sleeve. "It sure is good, and it wets the whistle."

Still gasping, Doug agrees. They take the tame stuff upstairs for the rest of the family. Colleen has the repast all ready to go. They sit around the table and chat, Doug tells Jim he's doing very well with the story, and the recording is pretty close to perfect. Doug asks Jim if they should continue or wait until tomorrow. We can continue for a Big while I'm warming up to my story, and Jim holds up his cup and says that the cider has revived him. Doug knows what cider Jim was referring to. After the repast, they all pick up and gather outside on the patio to continue the story.

"Where was I now?" Jim muses for a moment when Jeff speaks up.

"Grandfather, you left off where Billy was putting away the documents."

"Thanks, Jeff. Now to continue."

Billy stashes the copies of the documents; in case he's killed or imprisoned along with a letter explaining what the evidence means. The evidence will implicate several Government officials (called the Five) in stealing property and mining the power crystals from the mine they took. After Billy puts the documents into a safe place, he goes back to base to present the evidence he has to the Captain.

"Captain, these men are responsible for creating the Sky Pirates. They're bigger thieves than the pirates, and they should be arrested and made to return the land and the money they stole back to the family they stole it from", states Billy.

"Billy, I cannot deny what you say is true, and we should do as you say. But the men you are implicating own this world. There's nothing you or I can do to bring them to justice. They own the justice. You need to keep this to yourself, or they'll make you a target." observed the Captain.

"I see, only the privileged get justice. For your sake, and the men in the Secret Police, I'll keep silent, but I warn you. If the possibility comes up and I can arrest them or even one, I will!" states Billy.

"Billy, let it go, now get back to finding the Princess and capture her." commands the Captain.

Billy stands to attention and salutes the Captain then leaves the room. Billy locates Bruiser, the one man he can trust. Billy tells him all that has transpired.

"Why're you telling me this, Billy?" asks Bruiser.

"Because Bruiser, I'm now too dangerous to live, I know too much. If they find out I told you, your life will not be worth a dead crystal. You'll not tell anyone. I just wanted one person I trust to know the proper story. Now Bruiser, punch me in the face as hard as you can, so everyone can see you do it. Then stomp out of here angry," said Billy.

"If you say so." Bruiser punches Billy right in the face knocking him out. Bruiser stomps out of the barracks where they are. Then a few of the recruits come over and help bring Billy around. Billy tests his jaw to see if it's still in place.

"Sir, what happened?" asks one of the recruits.

"None of your business recruit," said Billy with some heat.

Billy Leaves the barracks and heads for his plane, he checks it out and takes off without telling anyone and getting permission. At the same time, a small contingent of men is looking for Billy to arrest him. The Captain reported up to the authority's what Billy has found out, and his intentions. Billy is now an enemy of the state, and he needs to be arrested. As it is Billy is just one step ahead of the government marshals. Billy boards his plane and flies off and away from all his friends to protect them. Jim and his family should be safe since no official records are linking them to gather. Now to set out to find the Princess.

Billy realizes he'll need allies, and right now, Billy believes he can find one in the Princess and her men. There are Five men that need to be brought to justice for their crimes against the Princess's family. And to the rest of the world of Topaz. Capture them and publicly show the crimes they've done against everyone so they can be brought to justice. Billy still has a map showing all the places where the Princess might hold up. Billy has not guessed that the Princess has returned to the Zeppelin port at Mid-City that they had left. Billy flies on to one of the islands not far offshore to wait and see if the Princess will arrive.

At the port, the Princess manages to contact her men, bringing the money, planes, and supplies to the Zeppelin and loads them up into the Zeppelin's bays. Just before The Princess leaves the dock, they get an urgent report about public enemy number one, Billy Webber. He's to be shot on-site, and no questions will be asked. Billy has threatened the Five men of top government positions (Called the Five). The Princess calls all the men on the intercom "we'll leave in 10 minutes so make everything secure. Helm contact ground control and tell them we're leaving."

"Yes, Princess."

In ten minutes, they are lifting up and away from the port; the Princess is pacing back and forth, trying to think like Billy.

She walks to the map on the wall. She sees the nearest island they had used in the past.

"Helm, when we're clear of the port head for this island, and I hope he'll be there," said the Princess.

Billy gets to the island in his plane; then, he decides to wait for a week then move on to the next island. Billy hopes he can catch up to the Princess. Two days later, Billy hears the motors of a Zeppelin overhead and decides to take cover. Billy has already hidden his plane in the brush and covered it over. If the Secret Police are coming in for a landing, he can hide until they leave. As it turns out, he realizes it's the Princess's Zeppelin which lands. The Princess is the only one to leave the Zeppelin.

"Billy, please come out. I know you're here. I saw the news bulletin about you. You're as hunted as I am, for much the same reason." pleads the Princess.

Billy steps out from the shadows not far from where the Princess stands, as Billy speaks, the Princess jumps with a start.

"Billy, you caught me off guard," said the Princess.

"Sorry, but when you are running for your life, one needs to be cautious," said Billy with a smile.

"You believed me, and you checked up on what I said. Why, Billy?" pleads the Princess.

"You were telling me the truth, and it piqued my curiosity. I had to verify at least to myself if you're stringing me along, or if it was real. When I found the evidence, I took it to the Captain. When he looked over, he told me to leave his office and how absurd all this is. I realized he'd report this up, and

I'd be arrested not long afterward. I fled and came here hoping you'd stop by here."

"According to the news, you are wanted for killing your Captain and others, you didn't do that, did you?" asks the Princess.

"You know me better than that, Princess, I don't kill unless forced. Now I need you and your men if I'm going to live long enough to bring these men to justice. Will you join me?"

"Join you! No, you'll need to join me!" demands the Princess.

Billy walks up to the Princess, sweeps her up into his arms, and plants a kiss on her lips. At first, she is trying to push Billy away, and soon she is holding on to him and returning his kiss. Billy's legs feel like water at this time, and his heart is racing. When they finish, the Princess steps back and slaps his face. "You don't ever do that!"

"Well?" asks Billy.

"Well, what?" asks the Princess.

"Will, you and your men join me to bring these men to justice?"

"Yes, only because it'd suit me to see them taken down. Alright, we'll follow you."

"Good, I need a couple of men to help me load my plane on to your Zeppelin."

Vantessa and Billy board the Zeppelin. To get the men to load Billy's plane onboard. Once that's done, Billy asks the Princess where they could go for now to plan the next moves.

"What next move, Billy?" queries the Princess.

"My next move is to train your men to fight, and see what

they can suggest to come up with to trap our first crook."

"If you train my men to fight as we do, they'll rebel against us, Billy."

"Princess, there're better ways to rule than using fear, Loyalty and friendship are at the top of my list."

"Ok, do it your way, and when it fails, we'll do it my way." said the Princess.

"As you say, Princess. Now call your toughest man here so I can meet him. He and I are about to put on a show for the crew," said Billy.

"Sure, I already beat him; why do you think he's not running the show here." complains the Princess.

Except for personnel needed to keep the ship on course, all the men and a few women show up on the hangar deck to see a demonstration. And to hear Billy's plan for what the future may be for them all.

A large man shows up as requested, the men on board the Zeppelin call him Big John. He's near twice the size of Billy.

"The Princess sent me and told me to do whatever you ask."

"My name is Billy, may I have yours?"

"They call me Big John."

"I can understand why John, you sure are a big man. I want you to do the best you can to kill me."

"WHAT?!!!" exclaims John.

"You heard me; I want you to try to kill me. To make it more interesting, here's a bag of fifty gold coins. You can have it if you can beat me." said Billy.

"I don't know Billy the Princess told me not to hurt you,"

complains John.

Billy looks up at the Princess, and she stands up and tells Big John to do his best to kill Billy. Big John smiles an evil grin and slams his fist into his other hand. John wants revenge since the Princess bested him in the saloon. Some time ago, in front of all those men. Billy sizes up John and knows he'll do his best to try to kill him. They circle each other looking for openings. Billy feints to the left and quickly turns to John's right side and pinches a nerve in John's leg, causing it to go numb, and it makes John limp. John realizes that Billy can do what the Princess did to him, so John slows his attack and tries to think about it. Billy moves in, and John manages to land a punch to Billy's chest, knocking him to the ground, and it knocks the wind out of him. Billy is trying to catch his breath, as John advances toward Billy, he raises his foot to stomp on Billy's head. Billy rolls out of the way and numbs John's other leg causing John to become immobile. Billy walks up behind John and pinches John's neck knocking him out.

The people in the gallery start laughing when Billy holds up his hands for silence. I'd not laugh at Big John; when I've finished teaching him, he'll take any ten of you. John is going to be my Lt. Then he is going to help me train you! Everyone is now quiet, and The Princess gets up and leaves. Billy follows her with his eyes. Billy reaches down and wakes up John and removes the numbness from his legs. Then offers him a hand up; at first, John is hesitant, fearing to be put back down.

"John, you have nothing to fear from me or anyone else,

you fought a good fight. I was just better, that's all. You're to be my Lt. I'm going to teach you how to fight, and then you're going to help me teach these other people in the gallery above to fight. Would you be interested?" asks Billy.

Billy helps John to his feet.

"Yes, I'd like to learn how to fight as you do."

"Thanks, John, we've got a lot of work to do to get everyone into shape, can I count on you?"

"Yes! You teach me how to fight as you do, and you can count on me!" as John's thumbs his chest with his closed fist.

"We'll start training tomorrow, same time," asks Billy.

"I'll be here, sir", states John.

Billy shakes John's hand and walks off after the Princess. Billy catches up to her on the bridge of the Zeppelin. The Princess turns toward Billy.

"You know how to fight better than I do, you didn't hurt John. You merely disabled him. Would you teach me as well?" she asks.

"Princess, I'd be overjoyed to teach you what I know. I assume you have a private place where you'd want my instruction?" asks Billy.

"Not yet, but I will."

"Princess, when you're ready, let me know. I'll be happy to teach you."

Billy starts to turn away and head to his quarters when he stops and asks a question.

"You do have an information-gathering network in place; do you not?" asks Billy.

"I do. Why do you ask?" puzzles the Princess.

"In the morning, when I've come up with the proper

questions, I'd like your people to start gathering the information I'll need to do the coup I have in mind."

"A coup, on who?" queries the Princess.

"I'll reveal all in time, Princess; I'll give you what I want to know about; for the time being."

Without asking permission, Billy turns and leaves the bridge, which infuriates the Princess to no end! Billy stops at the door and hears an object hit the wall next to the door. Billy smiles to himself as he walks out the door to go to his room.

The next day Billy and Big John meet, and Billy starts his instruction on how to fight using pressure points on the body. Billy also teaches John how not to get riled up while fighting. In a month, Big John learns to fight the right way and keep his cool. In walks one of the crew and hands Big John a note. John stands there looking at it and opens it up. Then he turns it all about with confusion written all over his face.

"What's wrong, John?" asks Billy.

"I can't read." stammers John.

"I see if you like, I'll read it for you," said Billy.

"Billy, it may be private."

"Ok, I promise I won't look at it when I read it to you."

"Are you sure?" quires John.

Billy almost cracks a smile but manages to keep a straight face, so John hands over the note.

"John, the Princess, would like to see you in an hour. You just have time to shower and put on a fresh set of duds." Billy hands back the note. "John, you need to learn how to read and write, so you can add more tools for you to use in a fight."

"How do words become a tool to fight with?" asked John.

"In time, you'll see it. Also, words can do more damage than a gun if applied properly."

"If you say so, Billy."

"I do, John, and I give you my word, to teach you what I can. Now starting tomorrow, we'll begin to teach others how to fight. Now off with you; you don't want to keep the Princess waiting."

An hour later Big John arrives at the bridge where the Princess is waiting for him. John enters the room and salutes the Princess.

"You sent for me, Princess?"

"Yes, John, I did. I wanted to get your assessment of your training."

"Billy is teaching me how to fight, and he's going to teach me how to read and write."

"If you can't read, who told you what was in the note?" asks the Princess.

"Billy did Princess; he promised he wouldn't look at it when he read it to me."

The Princess turned away from John for a few moments to compose herself.

"John, do you trust Billy?"

"Yes, Princess, I do. I trust Billy with my life, and now I'd give my life for his."

"John, would you give your life for me?" she asks.

"Yes, Princess, but not for the same reason you'd want, you

see Billy has inspired me to help people, and help my enemy. You inspire with fear; Billy does it with friendship and honor."

"I see, thanks, John, for being honest with me, you may leave me now."

John turns to leave and then turns back. "Princess, Billy Loves you, and you love him. It's a Big hard to miss. Don't let him getaway. Hold fast to him; he's the best thing to happen to you. Don't try to use force or your famine whiles it won't work with Billy. You can easily win him over with love and your trust," said John.

John then leaves through the door. Leaving the Princess to ponder all that John had said. From that day forward, the Princess attends all of the practices so she can watch Billy. Billy asks the Princess if she'd like to teach the other two women how to fight. The Princess steps in, to just do what Billy asked. The Princess teaches the two women how to fight.

During off-hours, you'd find Billy and John in the mess deck where Billy teaches John how to read and write. After a while, John is devouring any book; he can lay his hands on. Billy starts to show John numbers. Everyone sees a significant change in John's attitude. Others came to the sessions to also learn schooling. Billy turns some of the people over to John to teach. At first, John doesn't want to do it until Billy tells him if you're going to be a leader, you must be able to teach. John jumps in with both feet and starts teaching. Billy is always around to lend a hand or an explanation.

The Princess teaches the women, and Billy with John teaches the men. At a later date, the Princess comes to

Billy with the information he requested some months ago. At first, the information seemed pointless; then, as more information is accumulated, it begins to make sense. Soon Billy starts formulating a plan. On how to take down the Five biggest men of the world. The next morning, Billy presents the idea to the Princess. What Billy proposes is that they find a printing company under the radar or an abandoned print factory. Billy explains that they cannot use force to take the Five down they'll have to apply truth to do it. We need to put out so much truth that the Five will come out of hiding, and this'll enrage the people to incite a riot or a rebellion. For the people who can't read, we'll need a way to broadcast that message over the radio.

The Princess is about to reject the idea when she remembers what John said to her about following Billy. She looks him full in the face and realizes that John is right.

"Billy, I'll support you on this, and Billy, my name is Vantessa."

Billy looks up and smiles, "thank you, Vantessa! That's a pretty name; I like it."

The Princess feels a warmth in her face at Billy's words.

"We need to find the equipment to start our war, I'll bring in John, and can you select one of the women to work with John. They're going to be our front."

"What do you mean, our front, Billy?"

"Well, it's synch that neither you Vantessa nor I can walk into a town and not be arrested, so we'll need two people we trust to speak in our stead."

"I see what you mean Billy, I'll pick Glory, besides she likes John."

That evening, Billy, Vantessa, Glory, and John, meet in the brig with guards posted at the far end, so Billy can outline what he wants John and Glory to do. First off, they need a place to publish an underground newspaper, and then locate some radio equipment that they can install onboard the Zeppelin.

"Ok, John and Glory, I need for you to pose as business people! First, let's see what you can find as far as abandoned newspapers. I don't want to purchase it; I just want to use it. If we can, I want to keep it under the radar. So, buying a place would put a target on us when we start printing if we do this under the table they won't know where to look. So, we can remain safe for a time." explains Billy.

"Billy, how will we distribute the papers?" asks Vantessa.

"I'll take care of that end of it. If you were to use people to do that, they'd become unwitting targets", said Billy.

"Billy, you just want Glory and me just to locate a place." asks John.

"Yes, John, and the more remote, the better."

Glory chimes in. "What am I suppose too do?"

"Several things Glory, we want you to act as John's assistant. You'll work as a distraction and keep John out of trouble," said Vantessa.

"I can do that." states Glory as she eyes John.

"After you locate a newspaper factory, I want you to locate and purchase broadcasting equipment. See if you can locate any out of work radio newscaster," said Billy.

"How much time do we have, Billy?" asks John.

"The sooner, the better John. Now get some business

clothes on, and we'll be setting down in two hours. Glory dress for the part, Glory I need for the men to be distracted." says Billy.

"Not to worry, Billy We'll see to it," said Glory as she bats her eyes.

Two hours later, the Zeppelin lands at Billy's old airport. To drop off both John and Glory, in the middle of the night. Billy gives John the key to his hangar so they have a place to stay while they set about their tasks.

They get up to the loft where Billy's room is, and they look around, and it's still reasonably clean; Glory sees one bed and a lumpy couch.

"Who gets the bed?" asks Glory.

"Who do you think!" said John. I'll take the couch."

"Are you sure, John?" wheedles Glory.

John looks at her for a moment and turns very red with embarrassment. Seeing his predicament, Glory laughs. Glory likes John. John has yet to figure that out. All his life, women have feared his size and stayed away from him. Glory is the first woman he has had to work with as an equal. They finely go to sleep and wake up late in the morning. They dressed up as instructed. Glory carries a notebook to make notes on. They hail a taxi and travel into town to find a land agent to see if any abandoned newspapers are in the offering. At the office of the largest land agent for the island nations, John and Glory ask about small and large printing shops.

Chapter

24

The land agent offers to show them around a few of the abandoned shops. John and Glory go with the agent, and none of the places are what John is looking for, but Glory notes the addresses and possible capabilities for printing. They've seen and gone through three of the printing businesses large and small. Glory turns on the charm and gets a list of the other three big islands where other printing facilities are located. The agent takes Glory's attitude as a possible sign to fool around. He places his hand on her knee, and Glory puts her hand at the base of his neck at the shoulder, then pinched his neck, and he starts writhing in pain.

"Don't touch the merchandise, do you see the man I came in with? If he saw you touch me, he'd rip your head off and feed it to you. I'll forget this, and you'll forget us. If not, you'll feel this pain for the rest of your life, do we understand?" hisses Glory.

The agent nods his head. Glory removes the pain by

touching the same area "we won't be back."

"Good!" stammers the agent.

Glory and John leave the office. John asks, "what was that all about?"

"He got a bit frisky with me, and I taught him some manners. I made him want to forget all about us. I have a list of all the publishing business addresses that have been abandoned. Now tomorrow we'll get the broadcasting equipment." said Glory.

"Did you say he tried to get friendly with you?" asks John with some heat in his voice.

"Yes. Why do you ask John?" as Glory tilts her head and bats her eyes at him.

"I'm going to go back and straighten him out," said John.

Glory is thrilled that John is angry, that means he likes me. "Leave him alone, John; it served its purpose. I have the lists, and he'd rather not see us anymore." Purrs Glory.

"If you say so, Glory, but the next guy who gets fresh with you, I'll tear him apart," John says with some heat in his voice.

Glory is secretly overjoyed at John's words. Glory reaches over and takes John's hand, and John is at first shocked, and then a warm feeling comes over him. No girl in his entire life had ever taken his hand. They returned to Billy's hangar, with a sack of groceries. Glory is going to make the meal, in hopes of impressing John. She makes what we'd call chili here on our planet. As it turns out, John loves her chili. John has three large helpings.

"Glory, this is great; it's just like my mom made it when I was a kid." complements John.

Glory glows from the complement. It does her heart good to please John in any way.

"John, who's going to do the broadcast from the ship?" queries Glory.

"I don't know; I never gave it much thought yet; do you have a suggestion?" asked John.

"We're going to need a disk Jockey type of person John, or no one will listen to the broadcast. We'll need to find someone with some fire or some sort of flash and dash." muses Glory.

"Who'd you suggest, Glory?"

"I don't know yet. Maybe when we locate some equipment tomorrow, we can ask for any DJ's who needs a job."

"That sounds good to me. I just hope he'll want to come with us after we find him."

They turn in for the night. Early the next morning, Glory gets up and fixes breakfast for them. John does breakfast justice by eating his fill. John complements Glory on the great breakfast she made.

"Glory, you'll make a man a great wife someday."

"Be careful of what you say, John or a girl may misunderstand and think you're making a proposal and accept it." Purrs Glory.

John splutters, spraying food everywhere. "What?!" Glory laughs and thinks to herself; you'll be my man before I'm through with you, John.

John says nothing, and they get dressed so they can locate the broadcast equipment. Hopefully, a DJ to go with it. John and Glory make their way to a radio shop to make inquiries about purchasing used broadcast equipment, and possibly locating a DJ, they can hire. They chose a local radio place, and they find nothing to buy. John asks the man behind the counter where they can go to get that kind of broadcast equipment.

"You can't buy that kind of equipment without special permits from the government. Now a station over in the next city called Appleton shut down my friend's broadcast station because the government didn't like what he was broadcasting. You may be able to buy his broadcast equipment."

John, thanks the man. John and Glory rent a car so they can drive over to Appleton. In Appleton, they ask around for the location of the broadcast studio. They're considering on purchasing the station. They received directions from one of the pedestrians on the street. They follow the direction they were given and drive there. John and Glory get out of the car. And walk up to the door to go inside, but it is padlocked closed. They decide to leave when a wild-eyed man steps from the alley to confront them.

"So, you're the ones who shut me down, are you?!" said the man.

"No said John; we came here to inquire about buying the equipment."

"It's not for sale." states the wild man.

"Who are you?" asks Glory.

"I was the owner until I spouted off about the Five biggest crooks on our world. Then they shut me down and stole my equipment." huffed the wild man.

"Interesting. Said John. How'd you like to get your equipment back?"

"I would!" said Jack Ripper, "But How?"

"You leave that to me. One other question, do you know of a DJ who is out of work?"

"Big guy, you're looking at him!" said Jack Ripper.

"Very good," said John. John introduces himself and Glory to Jack Ripper.

"What do we do for now?" muses John.

"I guess I need to make a call for a pickup, and we'll help you get your equipment back." John walks off to the side of the building, away from Jack and Glory. John takes out a radio and calls the ship.

"Calling Sky-1, this is Big John, calling Sky-1, this is Big john, please come in."

"Big John, this is Sky-1; Billy here have you picked up the package?"

"I have it to hand, we also picked up a professional broadcaster, over."

"Thanks, John, good thinking on your feet." Complements Billy.

"I can't accept that praise Billy; Glory is the one who came up with that one."

"I understand, a good job just the same," says Billy.

"Sky-1 follow the radio signal to get my location, how soon can you get here?"

"We're an hour out; will that be soon enough?" asks Billy.

"Yes, Sky-1, are you going to wait for nightfall?" queries John.

"Yes, John, I assume that'll be at a discount on the purchase of the broadcast equipment?"

"That it will Sky-1. Over and out," said John.

From around the corner, John can hear Glory in a loud voice, telling Jack to get his hands off her. John rounds the corner and sees Jack trying to paw her, which makes John mad. John reaches out and pinches Jack's neck instead of ringing it. Jack drops off to sleep.

"That should keep him out of trouble for a while, said Jack."

"Thank you, Jack! I had my hands full keeping him at bay," said Glory.

Jack realizes that she could've put Jack to sleep as well as he did, but John didn't say anything. It made John feel needed, and he liked the feeling. For now, they decided to go to a café. John picks up Jack and carries him to the car and places him in the back seat. They soon locate a restaurant and get something to eat. Then they'll wake up Jack, and see where they can go to wait out the rest of the day. That night the Sky Pirates fly over the broadcast station and dropped men down to raid the building of its broadcasting equipment. In two hours, all the equipment is taken up into the Zeppelin along with Jack. The next morning John wakes up Jack.

"We've got your broadcast equipment on board. Now we require you to put it back together, so you can broadcast to the world again, Jack", says John.

"What if I don't want to help you?" replies Jack Ripper.

"We'd just drop you off anywhere, Jack." John implies.

"Are we moving?" asks Jack.

"Yes, we are Jack, follow me." John leads Jack over to the

hangar area and opens a port, "take a look."

"Oh my, we are way up here, where are we?" asks Jack.

"That Jack is a secret. A moment ago, you indicated that you want off or won't help us. We'll drop you off, right from here." said John with a straight face.

"You'd throw me out of this Zeppelin from up here?" asks Jack with fear in his voice.

"Without hesitation, Jack. Oh, by the way, if you touch any of the women on board without their permission. The same thing will happen to you, especially if you touch Glory or try to." said John with some sternness in his voice.

"I understand, lead me to the equipment, and do you have a place where I can set it up?" asks Jack hesitantly.

"See Jack, how easy it is. Think of it this way; now you can broadcast all the truth about the bad guys. I'll get you a couple of helpers to help you set up your equipment. Now how long will it take before you can broadcast?" queries John.

"Maybe a couple of days," responds Jack.

"Good I'll tell the powers that be, you'll be able to broadcast in a couple of days."

John walks away to report to Billy and the Princess. John enters the bridge and finds Glory and the Princess in a quiet conversation. John stands at attention for a few minutes before anyone decides to take notice of him.

"What did you want to report John?" asks the Princess.

"I talked to the DJ we brought on board, and he indicates that the radio will be operational in two days," states John.

"Very well, you can find Billy on the hangar deck going

through the planes we purchased. You may leave us, John."

"Thank you, Princess." John then turns and leaves the room.

The Princess turns back to Glory. "How goes your campaign with John?"

"Not bad, he's jealous of me, and he goes out of his way to protect me. He even treats me like a lady. He even has compared my cooking to his mothers, and I find it gratifying that it's at least comparable."

"I'd say Glory, you have John where you want him, so when are you going to marry John?"

"I'm not sure, I think he is too shy to ask me, and if I wait, he may never pop the question."

"Well, Glory, you should ask John to marry you."

"Is that proper?" asks Glory.

"Who says it isn't. Glory go get your man." giggles the Princess.

"Princess, who'll marry us?"

"Billy will." The Princess laughs.

"How he has no authority to perform a marriage," says Glory.

"He will when I make him the captain of this ship." laughs the Princess.

"Princess, if you do that, you'll lose control over the whole outfit."

"I know, but I'll gain more in the long run." purrs the Princess.

"How so?" asks Glory.

"I'll get Billy in the end. Besides, everyone goes to him anyway; this'll formalize it, and one other thing. It'll make

Billy susceptible to being married."

"Good luck Princess, I'm going to go get my man."

"You can do it, Glory; I have faith in you." laughs the Princess.

Glory leaves to find John so she can nail him down to being married. The Princess turns the bridge over to the watch and goes in search of Billy in the hangar. The Princess finds Billy looking over the last plane, and he's happy with what he has seen.

"Billy, may I talk to you?" asks the Princess.

Chapter

25

Billy jumps down from the plane and faces the Princess. Billy is looking at her and wondering what she's going to say. "Yes, Vantessa, may I help you?" asks Billy.

"You're right about how you handle people, and I think you'll make a better Captain than I do. Will you accept that position for now aboard the Zeppelin?" asks Vantessa.

"Ah, Ah, I'm not sure I should, after all, you stole it and now own it." stammers Billy.

The men on the hangar deck yell at him, "say YES!"

Billy turns very red in the face, "Ok, but only until we finish what we've set out to do, then the Princess will be your captain again." states Billy.

The Princess watches Billy as he flounders about the answer. *Thinking to herself, I'll make you mine yet, Billy. John was right about you. Now I can see that you do like me, and that will do for now.* The Princess considers.

Everyone starts cheering that Billy is now the captain of the Zeppelin. Billy sets off to meet the DJ and have a conversation with him. Close behind him is Vantessa. Billy and Vantessa enter the broadcast room where the DJ, Jack Ripper, is setting up his station. Jack looks up and sees Billy and the Princess standing there observing him.

"You're them, aren't you? The public enemies of the state. Princess of the Sky Pirates and that Billy Webber guy? Stammers Jack.

"We're no more enemies of the state than you are, Jack," said Billy.

"then why am I here?" asks Jack the DJ.

"Very simple, we want you to broadcast the truth to the world about the Five," said Billy.

"Who's to say what the truth is, you or the Five?" asks Jack, the DJ.

Billy hands over one of the public files for one of the men of the Five in question.

"Look this file over, and you tell me if you think it's true or not?" said the Princess.

Jack, the DJ, takes the file and leaf's through it. "Is this for real? I mean, this is on the up and up?"

"Every word of it," said Billy.

"What I was broadcasting is true, and that's why the authorities shut me down. Jack said, talking to himself. I'll do it, but how? my equipment is not enough!"

"You've all your broadcast equipment here on the Zeppelin; you can broadcast from here." said the Princess.

"I can, but we need an antenna," explains Jack.

"I don't think that's a problem. chimes in Billy, the whole Zeppelin can act as your antenna."

"It might work at that, let me get back to work. Our first broadcast can be tomorrow if you like?" Jack says with enthusiasm.

"Great, one other thing, you cannot say we're in the air or on a Zeppelin. We'll become a target soon enough without telling them or letting them locate us. Let them assume we're on the ground and moving."

"You got it, Billy, and thank you for this chance," said Jack.

"You should thank the Princess; it's her Zeppelin," says Billy.

Jack Ripper turns to the Princess, "Thank you!"

"You can thank me best by putting out a good broadcast." said the Princess.

Billy and the Princess leave to go back to the bridge, On the way back the Princess holds Billy's hand as if it were a natural thing to do. This makes Billy a bit skittish, but he accepts it. Billy walks back to the bridge without complaint. The Princess was smiling inside as she kept a straight face.

"Billy, when are we going to start printing up all this information and put it out to the public?" queries Vantessa.

"I thought I'd take several people with me this evening and break into one of the abandoned news offices and see what we might do. The most ideal one is the one outside of town, it's small, but we can print up what paper they have on hand then move on to the next one that has been shut down", says Billy.

"Will we be able to get away with it?" asks Vantessa.

"I don't know. Maybe for the first few times, after that, they'll be watching for us."

"Then you be careful when you're down there," states

Vantessa.

"Believe me, Princess, I'll be careful. I've no desire to lose anyone, especially me."

Billy does something unexpected. Billy pulls the Princess to him and gives her a big hug, at first, she is going to fight it, then she returns it. She puckers up and closes her eyes, expecting a kiss. Billy looks at her face and smiles and then releases her to go off to collect his people for tonight. The Princess stands there a minute, realizing he is not going to kiss her. Vantessa feels the heat rising with her anger. She's not sure what she wants to do, kill him, or kiss him.

"Girl get a hold of yourself; you can't let him get under your skin." *she thinks.* Then Vantessa storms off back to the bridge.

Billy calls everyone to the hangar deck to see who he needs to go along on tonight's raid and work party. Everyone that's not doing something important assembles at the hangar deck. Billy asks who'd like to go with him, and everyone raises their hands. Billy rephrases the question.

"Who knows about turning on power?" One person stands up and says he knows how to do that. Billy asks another question, "who knows how to run a printing press?" No one answers. "Does anyone know of anyone who knows how to run a printing press?" "I do, said one of the women. My father used to run a newspaper until he was shut down by the authorities. They claimed he was subversive because he printed the truth about the Five."

"Would he help us?" asks Billy.

"I don't know if he would? I could ask him."

"Ok, where is he?" asks Billy

"Where are we at now?" asks the woman.

Billys open up a map and point out the town they'll be over and where the small print factory is located.

"I see, that's the factory my father once operated; we can go to his home and ask him," she said.

"Ok, pick one of these fine men to go with you, and go see your father. Then ask your father if he'd like to help us," said Billy.

The woman picks one of the men, and they change clothes, as it turns out the man knows how to fly one of the planes. They leave the Zeppelin and fly to the nearest airport where they can rent a car to her parent's house. The woman turns to her escort.

"If anyone asks, we're here to visit my parents so you can meet them as my boyfriend."

He agrees it's a good cover story as any. They reach Ginger's parent's house, and they knock on the door. Ginger's mom opens the door and invites them in. Ginger hugs her mother and introduces Herbert as her boyfriend. Ginger asks her mom where dad is.

"He's in bed, waiting to die. He has lost his fire and desire to keep going since they shut down his paper."

"May I go see him?" queries Ginger.

"Yes, he'd like to see you and your boyfriend." mom usher them into the bedroom.

Ginger turns to Herbert, "Stay here with my mom. I want to talk to my father alone first."

Herbert nodes, and stands nearly at attention next to her mother.

Ginger enters her father's bedroom. "What's this I hear that you've given up father?!"

"Ah, Ginger, you've come to visit, how nice of you." gasps her father.

"Get out of that bed, father, the world needs your skills!" commands Ginger.

"Yea, sure, that's why when I print the truth. I was shut down because the authorities said I was subversive." With some anger in his voice.

"Father, get out of bed and get dressed. We're going to go someplace. If you're not out here in the living room in five minutes, I'll have my boyfriend come in here and drag you out of here!" Ginger turns and storms out of the room. A few minutes later, her father comes out into the living room.

"Now, where are we going that's so important that you threatened me with this young man?"

"Mother get your coats, it's cold out, and we have a bit of a trip to make," says Ginger.

Soon they're in the car and floating down the road to the airport. When they get there, Herbert goes to the plane and puts in a call to the Zeppelin.

"SP-special, this is paper-one, over," said Herbert.

"Come in Paper-one."

"Sir, we need a pick up at the plant, is that possible?" asks Herbert.

"Paper-one we can be there in an hour, is everything alright?"

"So far, SP-special, I think you'll need to convince our package, of his worth," explains Herbert.

"Understand, when will you be there."

"One-hour, sir." We'll be driving there.

"We'll be there, paper-one. Thanks!"

Herbert gets everyone into the car and gets direction from Ginger as to where the plant is, Herbert drives them to the plant.

"Hey, why're we here? I don't want to see this place." says Ginger's father.

"Father, for once in your life, sit down and shut up! We're here to meet someone who's going to help you", commands Ginger.

Her father looks at his daughter; she has never spoken to him like that ever. Shocked, he sits down and doesn't say another word. When they arrive, the Zeppelin is a hundred feet above them. It's hard to see it in the dark. Soon Billy lands in front of them using one of the antigravity packs. Billys walks up to the car.

"Ginger is this the person you told me about?" asks Billy.

"Yes, sir, this is my father and my mother."

Billy takes the mother's hand. "It's my pleasure to meet you." Billy shakes her hand. Then Billy turns to her father. "You know how to run this paper factory?" asks Billy.

"Young man, I know every aspect of this factory. So, don't you question my knowledge!" said father with some heat.

"Sir, I'd never dare do such a thing. Would you come and walk with me? I'd like to explain more if you'll permit it." said Billy.

"Young man, why should I talk to you?" huffs father.

"Father, do you know who you're talking to?" asks Ginger.

Father looks at Billy for the first time. His eyes get big and say, "You're Him! Public enemy."

"Yes, I am, and I imagine you are too. Or why would they shut you down?" queries Billy.

"I haven't killed anybody as you have." said father.

"I've not killed anyone; I did try to arrest the Five for crimes committed against the people and wound up a public enemy. Now, as to why you're here. How'd you like to strike a blow for justice? What I need is a man who knows how to run this factory. Will you do it?" asks Billy.

Father Stops in mid-sentence and looks at Billy then his daughter. It's like a fire is being built in his heart, and he turns to his wife, then to Billy, Yes, I will!"

"You realize we'll not be able to do this but one time here."

"I know, but it'll be worth it!" says Ginger's father with glee.

"Good, I'll bring down more people. You just tell us what to do." Billy reaches inside his shirt and pulls a file folder out and gives it to Ginger's father. He reads a few pages, and he looks up at Billy, is this all true?" he quires.

"Every word of it," states Billy.

"No wonder they shut me down. Well, son, get those people down here we've work to do!"

"Yes, Sir!" as Billy snaps to attention. Billy looks up and sends a signal, and more people drop to the ground. Billy points out Ginger's father and tells them to follow his direction. Soon everyone is busy. The fire of Ginger's father is lit again, with a great deal of enthusiasm. They work through the night and into the late morning. Before dawn, the Zeppelin has moved off into the distance so as not to draw undue attention to themselves. They have the handBillys printed and bailed. Billy has Herbert, and a few men go to town and rent some trucks so they can move the leaflets off down the road to meet up with the Zeppelin and load it all onto the ship. Billy gets ready to leave and tells Ginger to return her parents to their home.

"Young man, you'll not leave us here; you'll place myself and my wife in grave jeopardy, so we're going with you." spouts Ginger's father.

"Ok." said Billy, we'll take you aboard."

Billy turns to Herbert, "you best return the car and pick up the plane then return to the ship."

"Yes, Sir." Herbert runs off to perform his task. Ginger makes sure her parents are put aboard and placed in a cubical of their own. Later, Billy and the Princess show up to visit Ginger's folks who helped put out with the handBillys. And thank them for their help.

"Son, are we going to be doing anymore printing like that in the future." Ginger's father asks Billy.

"My guess would be yes. Why? Would you like to continue to help?" asks Billy.

"Son, I've not felt this good in a while. Anything I can do to put those rats out of business", says Ginger's father.

"Very good then, I'll call for you later. I'll send one of the men to show you the way. I have other files like the one I gave you. So, you can write up the next set of handBillys that we can drop over a city," said Billy

Gingers' dad was rubbing his hands together. "Son, you got a deal!"

The misses looked up at the Princess and Billy. You could see the thanks in her eyes. Billy and the Princess smile back at her. As they get up to leave, Ginger's mom asks, "are you the notorious Princess I've heard about?" Ginger's mom asks.

"I'm not too notorious, but yes," said Vantessa.

"You're beautiful and kind," said Ginger's mom.

Billy and the Princess walk away. "I've never been told I was kind before. I rather like it," said Vantessa.

"Princess, I was taking notes of the conversation, and I agree with Ginger's mom."

"About what, Billy?"

"You're beautiful, I'm not sure about the kind yet," says Billy.

The Princess punches Billy in the arm, and he starts laughing. Billy turns to her and sweeps her up into his arms and plants a solid kiss on her lips. At first, she struggles, then relaxes and kisses him back. "Princess, I don't know where or when, but I'm falling in love with you." Billy lets the Princess go, and she's in total shock and doesn't know what to say. Billy takes her hand and leads her back to the bridge.

"Helmsman when everyone is on board and our last plane loaded up, go to eight thousand feet. Set course to the biggest city on this island. It's time to broadcast our news and drop a few handBillys on the population," said Billy.

"Aye, Aye, Sir."

Billy turns to another crewman. "Crewman, go to the broadcast center and find out how we're doing on getting the radio set up. see if it'll be ready to start broadcasting in the evening tomorrow?"

"Aye, Captain." The Crewman leaves to get the information.

Billy contacts Big John and has him bring Ginger's father up to the bridge. Soon the crewman with the radio information reports in that they'll be ready, and moments later, Big John shows up with Ginger's father in tow.

"Well, sir, are you ready to get started writing the rest of the handBillys?" asks Billy.

"Son, just give me the information, and I'll do the rest!" said Ginger's father with enthusiasm.

Billy walks over to a file cabinet and pulls out four more folders and hands them over to Ginger's father. "Here, this should give you the ammunition you need. If this all works, we'll pull down the criminals and restore law and order", said Billy.

"Son, we're going to do just that! "said the old man. He turns away to return to his sleeping area so he can work on his handBillys.

The Zeppelin is flying over a major city of that island tomorrow evening, and from a thousand feet in the air, Billy and the crew push the handBillys out of the bomb bay doors. And Jack Ripper starts broadcasting the new news about the Five men who've been stealing this world blind.

The uproar is so bad from the people that the army is called out to put down the riots. Then to start a search for the Zeppelin that is responsible. After the broadcast, Billy moves the Zeppelin away from the city and high into the air as he can safely go. Around nine thousand feet. The Princess tells Billy they should move off to the next town using the existing Zeppelin cargo routes that way, we'll not be so easy to track, they'll assume we're just a cargo ship.

"That's an excellent idea, Princess. Helm come about and fly at Five thousand feet, set the watch to make sure we don't run onto another Zeppelin", commands Billy.

The Princess is pleasantly surprised at Billy's complement. Most men of her acquaintance rarely complimented a woman for her thinking only on her beauty. Billy is not like most men. He is so sure of himself that taking a woman's advice doesn't hurt his ego. The Princess rather likes that. More and more, the Princess is beginning to trust Billy. One other thing about Billy, he never pays a complement without meaning it. Billy has been watching Vantessa, and he is starting to see a change in her. No deceit and no ruthlessness. It's being replaced by concern and loyalty and something else. That makes Billy uncomfortable.

Jeff speaks up, interrupting grandpa's talking. "They aren't going to get all mushy and stuff, are they?"

"You'll have to wait, Jeff, to see what happens in the story. Since you stopped the story, let's take a break. Talking is thirsty work." announces grandpa.

Everyone gets up and stretches. Then heads to the kitchen to get snacks and refreshments. It doesn't take long, and soon grandfather picks up his story where he left off.

Billy and the Sky Pirates make headway to the next big city to drop the next leaflet bomb and fill the air with the broadcast of truth, about the Five who're running Topaz. As people read the leaflets, some are enraged, some confused, some don't care. The Five have come together to try to put a stop to the Sky Pirates. They call out the Military and the police to put a stop to the goings-on that the Sky Pirates are causing. Marshall law is declared, and the people have to be inside their homes not long after dark. They're to throw away the leaflets they've picked up to read. They also declare the leaflets and broadcasts to be lies to subvert the government and the people's best interests. Then all the current public and restricted records have been picked up and destroyed. So, no one else can dig up the same information in the future. With the Military and the police activated, the first order of business is to bring down the Sky Pirates and bring in the public enemies for trial and execution. That order didn't sit well with Bruiser, Billy's friend. At that time, Bruiser thinks he'll have to defect and become a Sky Pirate again and join Billy, his friend.

As luck would have it, Billy has left the Zeppelin in his plane and sends a message to his friend Bruiser. Asking him to meet with him at his hangar. Bruiser leaves HQ as if to be undercover so that he can meet with Billy. Billy has a chat with Bruiser explaining what all Billy has discovered about the Five. Billy outlines his plan of attack, but not where or when they'll happen. Billy convinces Bruiser to stay with the Secret Police; he may need an inside man. Billy gets him to believe that he may need Bruiser in place to get Billy out of trouble if the need arises. Billy reminds Bruiser of the packet of information stashed in the hangar in the secret place if anything happens to Billy. Also, Billy tells Bruiser to leave it there until Billy is declared dead, this may be used to condemn the genuinely guilty people. Bruiser remembers and promises Billy that he'll not touch the packet unless it's necessary. Billy brings Bruiser up to date on what he has been doing. Bruiser said that it appears to be working. Instead of capturing you and the Princess, you're to be shot on sight. They want you and the Princes dead. Billy says goodbye to

Bruiser then leaves to fly back to the Zeppelin.

Upon catching the Zeppelin, Billy lands in the docking bay, and the Princess is there to meet him.

"Billy, where did you go?" asks Vantessa.

"I meet an old friend, who tells me that you and I are stirring things up a bit. We're to be killed, not captured."

"You could've been walking into a trap; you should've taken me along!" said Vantessa.

"It was no trap; besides, I know the area by heart. I could've led them a merry chase and thread the needle to lose them", explains Billy.

"You're insufferable!" she stammers and starts to turn away. Billy grabs her arm and pulls her to him. Billy soundly plants a kiss on her lips, and when he finishes, he said, "I love you too!" Her eyes got big, and she can't say anything.

Billy said again, "I love you!" The Princess ran off crying. "Now what did I do?" left in some confusion, Billy walks off to find Big John to see if he can explain the Princess behavior.

Before he leaves the bridge, Billy has the helmsman set a course for another city off the beaten path, because the Military will be waiting for them at the next big city. Billy figures that'll throw them off some if we bomb a smaller town. Billy knocks on the door to Big John's quarters and gets invited in. Glory is there as well. "I just left the Princess, and she ran off crying, all I told her was that I love her." Glory got a big smile on her face and left the room. Glory hurries to the Princesses' stateroom. John looks at Billy for a few long moments then burst out laughing.

"Hey! I didn't come here for your amusement." Billy said

sternly.

"John holds up his hands. "Ok, you told her that you love her?"

"Yes, and I kissed her too," said Billy, embarrassed.

"Was she scolding you at the time?" asks John.

"Yes, that was why I kissed her," said Billy.

"You're in big trouble, my friend." Laughs John.

"How So, John?"

"Now, she intends to marry you," John said with glee.

"Marry me? You're wrong, John! The Princess would never marry me in a lifetime." said Billy, unsure of himself.

"Ok, don't say I didn't warn you."

Billy beats a hasty retreat. Then proceeds to the radio room to talk about the next broadcast with Jack Ripper.

Glory finds the Princess in her room still crying.

"What did the big bruit tell you, to make you cry so?" asks Glory.

"He kissed me then told me he loved me, I've been trying for a long time now to get that out of him, and now he has. I'm so happy, I can't stop crying," said Vantessa.

Glory takes her into her arms and pats her head. "Now is the time to hook him and reel him in," whispered Glory.

"You think so?" asks the Princess.

"I know so," stated Glory. "He came to John and me and started asking questions about why you'd start crying. Right now, he's confused. He's asking John what to do next."

"What did John say to Billy?" asks Vantessa.

"Nothing much, John still doesn't know how women think. So, whatever he tells Billy, it won't help, now's the time to spring the trap. Just stay near him, he'll cave sooner than you realize."

"Ok, I'll do that, thanks, Glory!"

"Now I've something important to tell you."

"What is that, Glory?"

"I'm going to have a baby."

"Really! That's wonderful." The Princess stops her tears to hug Glory.

"Oh, no!" said the Princess.

"What's wrong?" asks Glory

"You and John have to leave the Zeppelin," demands Vantessa.

"Why?" asks Glory.

"I'm sure we'll have to fight to keep free, and I'll not have the child of my best friend in jeopardy. I'm going to have you dropped off where I picked up John so that you can be safe. Your husband will agree with me as well," said Vantessa.

"You're the only one I've told about this; I haven't told John yet," said Glory.

"I'll not ruin your surprise, but tell him soon, or I will," said Vantessa.

"Thank you for not saying, anything Princess."

"Glory, congratulations, and on your way out, send the man in the corridor off to find Billy, I must talk to him," said Vantessa.

Glory does as she is asked and then heads down to where John is. Glory is planning to pull the rug out from under John about her being pregnant.

Billy gets the message and returns to the bridge. "Princess, what did you need?"

Princess takes Billy to the map and asks that the course be changed for this island.

"Can you tell me why?" asks Billy.

"No Billy I can't, at least not yet. If you knew what I know, you'd do it without hesitation. I ask that you not pressure me to tell you. Please just trust me." said Vantessa.

"Vantessa you have my trust, we'll do it your way, unless something changes it," states Billy

"Helm come about and lay in a course for this island."

Billy gets ready to rescind his orders for Jack Ripper, the DJ, and the leaflet drop as Billy turns to leave.

"Billy, will you have dinner with me tonight?" asks Vantessa.

Billy stops to look at her, studying her if you like. then asks, "Formal or informal?"

"You may come dressed any way you like," she said.

"Alright, I accept your invitation. What time?"

"Six bells, alright with you?"

"That is three hours from now. I'll be there. Thank you for the invite."

Billy bows to her and leaves the bridge, and the Princess is in a flurry of movement. Vantessa contacts the cook in the galley. And orders a special dinner with all the trimmings to be sent to her room. Then she dashes to her room to find something to wear at dinner. I want to knock the eyes right out of his head. She says to herself. Billy manages to borrow a formal suit from one of the crewmen, and he shows up at the Princess's stateroom. With some coaching from one of the men, Billy manages to learn about formal dining and manners. Billy is going out of his way to impress Vantessa. A short time before the dinner, Billy arrives in all of his finery, and Billy knocks on the door to Vantessa's stateroom.

The Princess has her helper let Billy into the living area of her stateroom, while she finishes dressing. Anticipation is everything in an entrance, and she wants to do a grand showing. Billy pours himself a drink and is about to take a swallow just as Vantessa enters the room, and he nearly chokes on his drink. And his breathing is very heavy, and his eyes popped out of his head. Billy stammers, "Princess?"

The Princess stops and lets him look her over, and she is getting the effect she wants. She, too, is shocked when she realizes he's well dressed. And that he likewise offers to seat her. Billy, she knew she didn't have any formal dining manners, what happened? She couldn't have been more surprised or happier that he'd go out of his way to learn all this for her sake.

The dinner progresses, and Billy made many small mistakes, and Vantessa follows suit so as not to embarrass Billy. She thinks that she can teach him later. Billy loosens his tie several times as he progresses through the dinner. Billy is grateful for the crash course at manners that the crewmen taught him. Billy hopes that Vantessa doesn't get offended by his lack of upbringing. At the end of the dinner, Billy complements Vantessa on her dress and the dinner as he takes her hand. Billy turns to leave. "What no kiss?" she asks.

"Ah, no. If I kiss you, I may not stop, and that'd be wrong since we're not married." stammers Billy.

"I'm willing to take a chance if you are."

"Ah, no." and Billy beats a hasty retreat. Once outside the door, Billy leans against the bulkhead and takes off the tie and uses it to wipe the sweat from his face. Then he lets out a sigh. Billy rushes off to his room to collect himself.

The Princess smiles as she watches him leave, knowing that he cares for her. That is enough for now. Vantessa calls her helper to change her clothes for bed, the whole time Vantessa is dancing upon a cloud, and is happy for the first time in many years. The next day they reach the small town and drop the leaflet bomb on them, and Jack Ripper broadcasts his message of villainy of the Five. Then they move on before the military, or the police can catch them. True to Billy's word, they leave for the island Vantessa requested. This catches the military and the secret police off guard. They're expecting him at the next largest city, so they massed the troops and planes to catch them, but Billy and the pirates are a no show.

Several days later, the Zeppelin arrives at Big John's home town where Glory and John leave the Zeppelin. The Princess in tears for losing the best friend that she ever had. Billy said goodbye to John and gave him a packet of information and a lot of money to help set them up here on the island.

"Are you sure you don't need us, Billy?" asks John.

"Need you, yes, want you NO! I'll not be responsible for the death of a child. You can best help me by raising a good family. Glory can help you learn more about reading and writing."

"Alright, Billy, now when are you and the Princess going to tie the knot?"

"What do you mean, John."

"Quit beating around the bush Billy; you know you love her. Even a blind man can see that." admonished John.

"I'm not sure she loves me, John," says Billy.

John puts his hands-on Billy's shoulders. "Billy, if you let her slip away, you'll be forever kicking yourself. Vantessa is the best thing to happen to you, and you know it," says John sternly.

"If you say so, John."

"I do, now get the ship out of here before the police catch you." Billy shakes John's hand and wishes him well.

After the woman give Glory hugs and a promise to return for a visit, they all return to the Zeppelin and leave to make way to the next large island. Billy consults the information that Glory compiled about the abandoned print factories. Then Billy heads down to visit Ginger's father to see if he can run the printing presses at that next print shop on the list. He affirms that he can, all the print factories have the same machines, so all the printing presses are about the same. Billy returns to the bridge to talk to the Princess about the next stopover to print more handBillys.

Billy reaches the bridge and asks where the Princess is, the man at the helm points to her stateroom. Billy walks over and knocks on Vantessa's door.

"Vantessa, it's Billy; I need to talk with you if I may."

"Enter the door is unlocked," calls Vantessa.

Billy enters Vantessa's stateroom, and he sees Vantessa in shear sleeping clothes. Billy's face turns red, and he turns his head and body to face the door he just entered in.

"Woman put some clothes on!" demands Billy.

Vantessa has a musical laugh, and she pulls on a robe over her shear sleeping clothes.

"I'm covered." Vantessa laughs.

Billy turns around, and he's still blushing. "You're a cruel woman for doing that!"

"Why what you saw is it not pleasant to you?" questions Vantessa.

"Vantessa, I was brought up to respect women who respect themselves; you show Big respect for your person! How do you expect me to treat you any differently than a street Trollope." splutters Billy?

Vantessa is taken aback by Billy's statement. Most of the so-called gentlemen she has ever known would've tried to take advantage and find her sting to be painful for trying. Now she's confused and angry for being called a Trollope. Wondering if she has pushed Billy away, and now she's ashamed. Of what she has done.

"I'm sorry, Billy. That wasn't my intent to make you feel bad about me, will you forgive me?"

"I can, but no more of this kind of treatment at your hands," said Billy with anger.

"You have my word; I'll treat you with utter respect Billy. said a demur Vantessa.

"Good now that we've gotten past this, I have to talk with you about the next stop for printing."

"What did you want to talk about?" asks Vantessa.

"You had a great idea before about following the cargo routes. As we appear here and there, they may be starting to look for us in the cargo routes. Do you have any other ideas about what to do now?" queries Billy.

"No, Billy, I don't, a Zeppelin is rather large and slow, we'll be seen before we arrive. You caught them off guard with the last city we targeted. Now they'll stretch themselves thin trying to catch us. Whatever we do, it needs to be unexpected." said Vantessa.

"Great idea Princess, what would they not expect of us. How high can we go in this Zeppelin?"

"Not much above ten thousand feet may be less with some of our crew, like Ginger's parents."

"Could we go higher if we had a way to breathe?" asks Billy.

"I never thought of that Billy, we could go very high, but only for as long as we have time in the air tanks," said Vantessa.

"I'm getting an idea, Princess; I'm going to my room to work on it. When it's fleshed out some, I'll come and see you and tell you what my scheme is."

Billy walks off; the Princess is happy to be included in the say of what goes on. Even more pleased that Billy believes in her abilities. "I'll be patient; he'll come to me when he's ready." She thinks. Billy gets to his room and starts planning his next campaign against the Five rulers of Topaz as he sets in his room and mauls over his idea to make it possible to breathe at the higher altitudes. And keep everyone warm at that altitude. To execute one of his ideas, Billy hits on one that just might work. Kidnap the top ruler (s), but after you capture one or two of them, the rest will be harder to do. Billy walks back to the bridge to talk to the Princess.

"Vantessa, which of the rulers has the most influence over the others?" queries Billy.

"The one on the largest island, why?" asks Vantessa

"Why him?" asks Billy.

"He has the most wealth and the largest army, but if the other ruler's band together, they could overwhelm him, and take over Topaz," she stated.

"I wonder what impact would be if we start a war between them. You see, over the years, they've built a wall of mistrust of each other. If we exploit this right, we could start a war between them." states Billy.

"To what effect, Billy? Would that not involve innocent people getting hurt?" queries Vantessa.

"Not the way I'm planning it. All we need to do is create dissension between them, then suggest to them that they meet to iron out their differences. They'll show up at let's say at a summit meeting someplace neutral. An out of the way place. Then we kidnap all of them or most of them and fly away where we can convince them to confess what they've been doing or are now doing to the people." suggests Billy.

"That sounds like a good idea, but how are we going to get close to them, they'll expect something of that nature, and protect against it," said Vantessa.

"Very true, except that I've been on a detail to protect one of them during my time spent in the Secret Police. I can teach our men how to act and respond and how to dress and what to say. The more I think about it, the better I like it." Billy muses.

"Ok, let's do it your way. Now, what do we do to get them to call this so-called summit?" asks Vantessa.

"We send a blackmail letter to each one, asking for hush money. Then I'll appear at the summit, where they'll capture me. Then our men who'll have infiltrated their security will rescue me. Then we capture the Five leaders and return to the Zeppelin."

"Oh, it's just that easy, is it? Your life won't be worth anything if you show up, and they capture you!" states Vantessa.

"It'll be that simple, risky, but that simple," says Billy.

"Then I'm going with you! Says Vantessa.

"No, you aren't! I'm going alone. I don't want you in danger, Vantessa, and besides, I can move better on my own."

"No, Billy, I'm going with you, it'll make things more tempting if I tag along. They want me just as bad as they want you. I can take care of myself. I got away from you, and the Secret Police did I not?" said Vantessa with some heat.

"Good point. Said Billy. Alright, you go with me, but only if you follow orders!"

"I will, then Vantessa mumbles, I will protect my investment."

"What was that?" asks Billy.

"Nothing, so how do we start this blackmail you suggested?"

"By sending a communication to each one, and include a copy of the documents I've collected against them. This should get their attention. Then we pick a meeting place, where they can ambush us."

"What? Ambush us! Aren't we going to get away?" asks the Princess.

"That's the beauty of it, they catch us, and we, in turn, capture them. We know how to fight, and our people will also know how to fight. Doing this will get us close to them so we can overpower them. Then we whisk them away here on to the Zeppelin. Then disappear," said Billy.

"That sounds easy in conversation; I hope it'll work?"

"Vantessa, do you trust me?" asks Billy.

"Yes!"

"I'm going to stop at the next town to send the bait to our Five fish, then you and I have a lot of work to do to train our people," said Billy.

"I don't like this, but if you think this'll work, then I'll do it," states Vantessa.

Billy rushes off to put his documents together. At the next town, as they hover, Billy drops down, flying his plane, and he goes to a telegraph center where he pays to have the communications sent off to the Five. Billy returns to the Zeppelin after he has sent off the telegrams. Billy leaves in a hurry before the police can be alerted to his presents. Back on board, the Zeppelin Billy heads to the bridge to plan where to meet with the Five. Billy pours over a few maps, and then Vantessa points out an island, where no one can get on or off without being seen. Vantessa points out that there is a hidden cave at the far end of that island. That'll be an excellent place to stash most of the pirates until we're ready to take action.

Billy gets into his plane and flies to the next town to send the Five the meeting location.

Billy returns to the Zeppelin and begins to train the men and woman who'll be involved in the kidnapping of the Five. Billy drills them in marching. Then both the Princess and

Billy train the people how to fight using the pinched nerve fighting style. The idea is not to kill; just disable the people you're struggling with. A week later, Billy has the Zeppelin land on the island. Billy and Vantessa take the trained men and women to the cave and get them situated. Billy shows them the plan that he has for them to perform; they're to sneak out and capture the Five's men and replace them until everyone has been replaced or until everyone is out of the cave and in position.

Then Billy and Vantessa will land and appear to fall into the clutches of the Five. Then at Billy's signal, we take over and capture the Five. Billy and Vantessa return to the Zeppelin high above the clouds to wait for their guests' arrival. The Five appear with their men early so they can get the lay of the land as they explore Billys people capture the Five's men. A radio call is sent saying the substitution has been completed. At noonday the Five land their Zeppelins and the Five have a small band of trusted men disembarks with them secure in the thought that they control the island, looking for possible ambushers. They only find a couple of people camping, which they arrest and put aboard one of the Five's Zeppelin. Over time the hidden pirates move out from their positions and surround the Five and the small band of men. During that time, Billy's men capture the men sent to the island. They remove the guard's clothes so they can wear them and use the communication devices the guards carried to let the Five know that they're in control. The men that Billy's people captured were placed in the cave stunned. So, they couldn't escape. Then the man guarding the prisoners called Billy, to let them know the stage is set.

Billy and Vantessa land on to the island and disembark Billy's plane. Billy has a large packet of paper, and he walks up to the Five men and addresses them.

"I have the evidence that I promised you, where's the money?" asked Billy.

"Men! Grab them and hold them!" said one of the Five.

Billy and the Princess are taken captive. As they stand there with guns pointed at them, the Five converge on them and take the information. One of them opens the packet and finds blank paper.

"Where's your evidence? I saw what you sent; it was authentic. Where's the rest of it?" As he slaps Billy in the face.

"You didn't think I'd bring it, along, did you? So that you'd take it at gunpoint, did you?" Said Billy.

One of the Five slaps Billy across the face again, leaving a red handprint where he was hit.

"Now Mr. Webber, you'll tell us where this evidence is, or I'll have this young lady killed right here." said the man with glee.

As one of the men grabs the Princess and puts a sharp knife to her throat, he presses the blade hard to draw blood.

"Stop, I'll give it to you," shouts Billy.

Then there is a ruckus out on the fringe, and before the Five realize, they're surrounded by the Sky Pirates. The Five are now the captives. The man holding the Princess soon finds himself on the ground writhing in pain, as Vantessa looks on and watches she kicks him for drawing her blood.

Billy looks on the Five. "I have the evidence to convict you of the crimes against the people; what do you have to say for your selves."

"That one, you are a fool to think that it'll get to court, and two, we're not who you think we are." said one of the Five.

"What are you talking about, you match the pictures of the men we want," said Billy.

"No, we just look like them. The Five were sure you'd pull something like capturing us, so the Five didn't come they sent us in their place. What you have are body doubles. If we succeeded in capturing you, we'd have been made rich. Now we're expendable," said one of the Five.

Billy turns to one of his men, "Take these men and head for the ship; this place is about to be bombed."

Billy and the rest of the men all head for the caves. The ones with planes take off to fly up to the Zeppelin. Just as Billy predicted, Zeppelins at a much lower altitude drop bombs that explode and spread fire in all directions. Billy and his men just keep ahead of the bombs once or twice a man lags behind and winds up being burned alive; this gives Billy and his men the incentive to keep running for the cave. In an hour, the whole island is covered in fire. Billy, Vantessa, and most of the men are safe in the cave. They wait out the day until the fire dies down. It's growing dark, and Billy with all the men and the Princess board the boat they had secreted away, and sail away from the island.

"How'd you know they were going to bomb the island?" asked Vantessa.

"Because, as the man had said, they're expendable, and if I had the evidence, what better way to get rid of everything.

"However, you knew Billy, you were right. It looks like they want a war, shall we give them one?" whispers Vantessa.

"On that, we can both agree. When we return to the Zeppelin, we can interrogate the Five body doubles we've caught. I'm sorry their guards died in the bombing, but that wasn't our doing."

"What do we do now, Billy?" asks Vantessa.

"I'll know more when I've had a conversation with the men we've captured. What I need to learn is which of the Five is the one in charge; from there, I'll formulate a plan to capture him," said Billy.

Billy stands looking out over the water, and Vantessa stands next to him, and she reaches down and takes his hand in hers. She too stares out over the water, realizing if it weren't for Billy, every one of them would've been killed in the bombing. Billy, though about removing his hand from hers, but he could feel her trembling. Her hand felt so small in his, so he gripped her hand back. Vantessa smiles.

An hour out from the island, the pirate Zeppelin drops down to intercept them, they load everyone on board and then wench the boat on board to store it for a later time. Billy walks Vantessa to her quarters, and then he kisses her hand that he had been holding, and he looks into her eyes.

"I was so afraid for your life today; my heart is overjoyed you're safe aboard your ship. I have fallen in love with you, and I realize that if you had died today, part of me would've died with you", states Billy.

Billy was going to say more, but the Princess put her hand to his mouth. "You can tell me all that's in your heart after we finish our war. So that you know, I feel the same for you as well." Vantessa steps into her room and closes her door. Vantessa is of two minds about the war; one is to find a place to live with Billy all to herself. Or reclaim her birthright. Both will get them killed in the long run.

Billy heads down to the brig to interrogate the Five men they've captured. "I see that your employers don't seem to care if you live or die. All your guards have been burned alive due to the bombing. I could've left you there. (Billy pauses for effect) Will you answer my questions?" demands Billy.

None of the Five men would say anything. Billy gets suspicious and asks for a hand scanner; Billy has one of his men run a scanner over the men. They don't find any beacons on them, but he finds other electronics on the right side of their bodies near their lungs.

"Get these men to the garbage chute now; they are carrying bombs."

His men inject the Five men with a sleep drug, and lug them to the garbage chute, and drop them out of the Zeppelin, on the way down the bodies explode.

"If we would've dropped our altitude, they would've caused some damage to our ship, what kind of monsters would kill people as if they're nothing."

No one answers, they're shocked and sickened by what they'd just seen. Billy leaves for his room to begin planning his next move. He learned something this night. Just how ruthless his adversaries are.

Billy leaves his room to see Vantessa. "Vantessa, I need to leave for a while. I have to make contact with a friend of mine. He works for the Secret Police, so I have to go alone to meet with him."

"Billy, you could be captured. Why must you go?" pleads Vantessa.

"My friend Bruiser, you remember him? Well, he'll not arrest me unless he has no choice. I'll make sure I don't give him that choice. He'll have some information I need, or he'll be able to get it for me." states Billy.

"Billy, you're safe here, why put yourself in danger?" asks Vantessa.

"Because Vantessa, I need the information. If all goes well, I'll get in and out of the city where Bruiser is stationed. And be back in a week." said Billy.

Vantessa grabs Billy's arm, with anguish in her voice and eyes. Vantessa pleads with him, but in the end, Billy goes off to see his friend Bruiser. Billy takes his plane and leaves the Zeppelin with orders to pick him up at the island that was just destroyed with fire in ten days.

Billy flies to his home town and lands at his hangar and parks his plane in front of his hangar in hopes that Jim Collins will remember his plane and come looking for me at my hangar.

Chapter

29

"Well, we need to stop for the night; the children are falling asleep. said Jim to his son. Jeff keeps yawning, and his sister is asleep."

"You're right, dad; come, wife, we'll take the children up to their rooms to sleep."

The children are carried up-stairs and put to bed. The grown-ups meet in the kitchen for a nighttime snack and some light conversation; then everyone is off to bed. In the morning, everyone meets for breakfast. Soon after, breakfast is eaten and cleared away. They decide to stay indoors due to the rain, so Doug sets up his recording equipment in the living room. "Ok, dad, we're ready to record," said Doug.

Jim looks around at his audience, takes a long drink of orange juice, and launches back in his story.

"Yep, that next morning, I spot Billy's plane." I go up to it and look inside. Then I walk back into my hangar and use the back door, and walk over to Billy's hangar. I carefully enter the back door and climb the stairs up to Billy's living area.

There on the couch, I see Billy sound sleep. I call his name, and he doesn't wake, so I put a hand on his shoulder and shake him awake.

"Hun, Wha... Oh, it's you, Jim."

"Who else would it be, young man?"

"Any number of people who'd want me dead."

"Oh my, why are you here then?"

"I need to contact Bruiser to get some information, and I hoped you'd be able to get a message to him for me," asks Billy.

"Won't he just arrest you, Billy?"

"No, he won't unless he has no choice. No, he is my friend, and if he can, he'll help me; at the very least, he'll send me on my way."

"Ok, so how do you propose to contact him? You realize he's high up in the Secret Police now."

"Oh, good, he got his promotion, said Billy. I was hoping that you two are still friends and that you could contact him to get him to meet you on some pretense."

"Where do you want to meet?" asks Jim.

"Tell Bruiser to meet me where we were on a stakeout at the main Zeppelin port. He'll know where to go", said Billy.

"Ok, I'll go see him tomorrow evening. We're having a poker night at his house, and he'll be there. I can pass this message to him there." said John.

"Thanks, Jim, I'm going to stay here and catch up on some sleep, it took me three days of flying to get here." Billy stretches and yawns.

Jim leaves by the back way and doesn't tell anyone Billy is

back. Billy sleeps most of the day away, and that night Jim returns with a chicken dinner from the dinner. When Billy sees the food, he realizes just how hungry he is. Billy gets out some dinner plates and pours some water from the tap, and both men sit down to eat dinner.

"Now Billy, suppose you tell me all about what you've been up to," asks Jim.

"Ok, Jim, I'll bring you up to date except for the last few days. Then that way, you'll not have to lie to anyone." Billy spends most of the evening going over what has happened; he leaves off the locations and dates for no other reason so he can protect his friend Jim from retaliation from Billy's enemies.

"Billy, I passed on the message to Bruiser just like you said. Bruiser indicated that he'd be there waiting for you", said Jim.

"Thanks, Jim. I'd best better get going I have a small distance to go tonight before I make it to the Zeppelin port to meet Bruiser."

"Good luck to you, Billy, you should marry that Princess of yours, you both sound like you have a soft spot for each other," says Jim with some amusement.

"Jim, I do like her, but as soon as she gets what she wants from me, I suspect she'll do away with me. Much like a black widow spider does her mate."

"Don't be too sure of that; I suspect she is laying a trap for you, Billy, but not the kind you suspect. I'd be willing to wager; she'd marry you then make your life interesting. Anyway, goodbye." Jim leaves Billy in troubled thought.

Marriage scares Billy. All that responsibility, best to leave that to other people. Billy gets around and finds his disguise in one of his bags; Billy then heads for his plane. Billy takes off to fly to the cargo port on the cost. Billy gets there and locates a room in one of the worst places in town. Then he puts on his old man disguise and hobbles to the port to wait for Bruiser to show up.

Late that night, Bruiser shows up with a couple of his men, and when he reaches the spot, he tells his men to continue and look for Billy. Bruiser then sets down next to the old man, turns to him, and holds up a picture of Billy.

"Old geezer; have you seen this man on this dock?" asks Bruiser.

Billy in a disguised voice, "Now let me see, no, I haven't seen that man here since I sat here."

"Ok, Billy, what do you want?" demands Bruiser.

"I wasn't sure you'd remember this disguise," stated Billy.

"Are you kidding? I saw you right off. I sent my men away so we can have a chat. What is it you want?" demands Bruiser.

Billy hands Bruiser back his picture, along with a picture of the Five. "Can you tell me which one is the main man in charge, and where I can find him?"

"I could, but why do you want to know?" demands Bruiser.

"Do you remember that packet of information I told you about, it contains evidence against the Five, it shows how they stole and killed to get to where they are. In effect, they were responsible for causing the Sky Pirates in the first place. I need to know where they are so I can remove them from power. Here is another packet I collected against them for killing all their people to just get at me. Read it, it'll make you sick," said Billy.

"Alright Billy, I'll get you the information, I'll get it to you myself, I'll have someone else pass it on to you. If you remember, I'm supposed to be looking for you and take you in under arrest," said Bruiser.

"Thanks, Bruiser."

"Don't mention it, now get out of here, you pirate." laughs Bruiser.

Billy takes Bruise's hand, then lurches off toward his room. On his way back to his place, Billy realizes that Bruiser told him that they were being watched and that he will be followed. Billy watches his back trail and soon locates his tail. Billy plays his role back to his room. Billy looks out the window and sees his tail across the street. Billy decides it'll be best to leave and find another place to occupy. Billy changes out of his costume and puts on another one. This disguise has a scar across his left eye and an eye patch. Billy puts on an old captain's hat, then Billy looks in a mirror and decides to darken his hair and hide one arm in his long raincoat as if he only has one arm. Billy collects his backpack and walks out the door in front of the tail and doesn't get a response from him because he is watching the door and the window looking for the old man.

Billy whistles as he passes, and walks down the street, searching for different quarters to stay in as he waits for the information Bruiser promised him. It takes Bruiser a couple of days to gather the information that Billy wants. He has information on all of the Five men. The more Bruiser gathers the more Bruiser suspects that Billy is right; these men must be taken down. Bruiser becomes determined to help in any way he can. That night at the port, Billy meets with Bruiser. Bruiser walks to the port, and he stops where he and Billy have met before. Bruiser doesn't see the old man and decides to wait. There was, however, a man with a scar across his face next to him. Bruiser chooses to wait when the man with the scar asks him for a light for his pipe as Billy puffs on the pipe and blowing out smoke.

"Do you have the information I asked for?" whispers Billy.

Bruise almost jumps with fright and then realizes it's Billy. "Ah, yes, I have it here." Bruiser pats his haversack.

"Good! says Billy, just leave it, and walk away; that fellow across the way is watching you and me."

Bruiser doesn't say another word; he drops the haversack behind him and stalks off as if he had been stood up. Billy continues to watch the tail and stands over the haversack on the ground. Billy drops his pipe and leans down to pick it up with the haversack and slips them onto his shoulder. Billy looks around and sees that the tail is gone. Billy makes his way back to his room. Billy is planning to depart as soon as he collects his bag. Billy gets back to his room and sees that someone is in his room by the light under his door. He walks up to see if he can listen to see how many people are in there when Billy hears a crunching sound and realizes that he is walking on broken glass. Billy turns and runs down the hallway to a window at the far end.

Behind him, his door opens, and two people in black are pursuing him. Billy dives through the 2nd story window and lands on the fire escape. Then down the stairs, he runs. Not far behind him, the two men in black are hot on his tail. Billy manages to get to the street. The men in black start shooting at him. Billy manages to run around the corner. Billy then steps into a doorway and waits for the men in black to follow him. Both men stop at the mouth of the alley, and one stares down one way looking for Billy the other one is watching in the other direction as the first man draws up next to Billy. Billy reaches out and pinches the man on the neck and renders him unconscious Billy then pulls him into the shadows. Billy watches the other man, and he then calls out to his partner and gets no response. After the third try, the man in black runs off to get help. Billy removes the man's weapons and moves off down the alley in the opposite direction. Billy takes an indirect route back to the airfield where his plane is. Billy preflights his aircraft, then gets in it to fly back to his hangar. Billy is soon in the air, and a few hours later, he arrives back at the home airfield as he's about to land. Billy sees lights on in his hangar. Billy decides to fly on; as he passes over the hangar, the lights go out.

Best to start the return trip back to the Zeppelin figures, Billy. Billy flies on, realizing that it's going to be a long flight. At the hangar, there is a squad of men waiting for Billy to land and enter so they can capture him. Bruiser is there with them he turned on the lights, then back off, to warn Billy he had a reception party waiting for him. Billy flies all night to the next airfield, puts on a disguise, and locates a room for the day to get some sleep. That night he buys some supplies and sets off to meet up with the Zeppelin. It takes Billy five days to get to where the Zeppelin is moored. Billy lands his plane and approaches the Zeppelin when a sentry challenges him.

"Halt, who goes there!" says one of Billy's men.

"It's me, Billy Webber."

"You don't look like him." challenges the sentry.

Billy realizes he still has on his disguise on, so he removes the mask and the makeup. "Is this better?" asks Billy.

"Yes, sir, Captain!" and the sentry steps aside.

"Good man, what's your name?" asks Billy.

"Chuck, sir."

"Chuck, you keep up the good work, you never know who may come along."

"Yes, Captain."

Billy heads on board the Zeppelin. Then he sends a few men to load his aircraft into the hangar aboard the Zeppelin. Billy calls up to the bridge to see when they can take flight; if it's not ready, prepare to do so. Billy had read over the information Bruiser provided him when he'd stop over for sleep along the way; Billy was formulating a plan to capture one or more of the Five. Back on the bridge. Vantessa meets with Billy and almost faints because of Billy's scar on his face due to the disguise. Fearing, he was hurt. Billy assures her he is unhurt and removes the scar. Billy starts to tell her about the information he has received from his friend Bruiser.

Billy tells her he is formulating a plan to capture the main man of the Five, based on the information he received from Bruiser. A few days later, Billy pulls Vantessa aside and tells her what he's thinking.

"Vantessa, I believe we can capture all the Five in one fell swoop. We need to get our people into each camp, so to speak", says Billy.

"How do you propose to do that?" poses Vantessa.

"We train ten people to be the best at fighting, to become part of the Fives security team. Then when the time comes, they drug the target and whisk them away. Then we meet with them to take custody of the Five."

"That's easy to say, so how'll you do it?" asks Vantessa.

"I'll train them!" said Billy. I was trained by the best the Secret Police had to capture you. As I recall, I did manage to arrest you." said Billy.

"You also remember I got away, right!" smiled Vantessa.

"I do remember, that'll have to be done carefully. Our people will be in constant danger, and I want them to have a better than average chance to survive; then capture their captive."

"When do we start?" asks Vantessa.

"Now, we need thirty people to start with. Now to see who we can train. Then we'll select the ten-best qualified with which to execute the plan," said Billy.

Billy assembles all the crew. "we're headed for an island for some intensive training. I need thirty volunteers to do that intensive training. All of you will get a chance to test if you like. I'll choose the candidates and then weed them out until I have the twenty people I need. Are there any questions?"

Someone from the back calls out. "What'll be doing?"

"That'll remain secret except for the ones who are chosen at the end of the training. Any other questions?"

No one says anything. "Good, Selections will start tomorrow

at 06:00 hours."

Billy then leaves the hangar area to go to the bridge to talk with Vantessa.

Billy goes to the door of Vantessa's stateroom and knocks on the door; the Princess opens the door and ushers Billy in.

"What do you want to talk about, Billy? By the way, I'm glad your back safe and sound."

"Thank you, Vantessa. I want to go over my plans for capturing the Five."

Billy outlines what he has in mind, "we need to pick the people who don't have a police record of any kind, then we'll train them how to fight, pick locks, and the like. Also, to be good with firearms. They'll infiltrate the Five's ranks, and at the right time, they'll render their intended person inert. Then spirit him away from their castle. Then we'll pick them up at the Five different locations."

"That sounds good, but how do we accomplish it?" asks Vantessa.

"With a great deal of ingenuity and luck," said Billy.

Vantessa goes over to her door. Then out on to the bridge, she rifles the file cabinet and returns with a couple of sheets of paper.

"Here Billy, these lists are what you need. It shows who has records, and who doesn't, it lists some of the skills that some of our people have. Like safecrackers, second-story burglars, and other criminal types, even a few assassins." The Princess hands over the sheets to Billy.

Billy looks over the information and asks, "how accurate are these lists?"

Vantessa looks at Billy, "They're very accurate, Ginger, when she was here, interviewed everyone, and confirmed them with police records."

"Good, we'll need the criminals to help us teach the ones who are not criminals. The way I see it, Vantessa, you work with the woman, and I'll work with the men. We'll sort out the people tomorrow and then begin training."

30

The next morning Billy and Vantessa meet with everyone on the hangar deck that is not necessary to fly the Zeppelin. Billy separates criminals from non-criminals. Billy had wanted thirty people to work with but soon finds that they have only twenty-Five people that don't have any kind of a record. Billy directs the men and woman without records to stand to one side. The rest he calls to attention. Billy calls out ten names from those who have records and dismisses the rest of the men and women. Of the ones selected, they are electronic, and mechanically trained people, safecrackers, and bomb experts.

"I've pulled you people from the crew to train your particular specialty to these people I put over there." Billy points to the group still at attention.

Billy walks over to the people at attention "at ease." Everyone stands at parade rest." Billy tells them they're going to be trained, very extensively. Billy points to the ten people standing to one side and explains that these aside from himself and the Princess will be your instructors.

"You'll learn to fight, unlock locked doors and safes, handle alarms and electrical systems, and mechanical systems. You'll be taught how to be a sniper and kill with just your hands. If any of you wish not to take part, you may leave now. Once you start, you'll finish the training and carry out the mission I have in mind. If you don't wish to do this, leave now!"

One person leaves the ranks. Billy looks around, "anyone else?" No one leaves. "Good, dismissed, and return in two hours your training will begin at that time."

Billy turns to the new instructors. "I'm sorry I cannot use you on the Five teams I need to make up, with police records you'd be discovered, and that would put you at risk. You can teach the others on the team how to do what you know. You may not be able to impart your skill, but the knowledge may just give them an edge to survive the mission, any questions?"

"Captain, why are we doing this?"

"That'll remain a secret until the last minute, any other questions?" "No. Good go brush up on your skills and see if you can make it easy to teach these recruits. Dismissed."

The next morning the selected group starts their training, running, jumping, climbing ropes, and fighting. The men are taught with the woman as far as the skills are taught. For the fight training, the women are pitted against the men with no holding back. In the end, the men are pitted against Billy himself. The woman goes up against Vantessa, then Billy, to test their limits. This is the procedure for each day. In the evening small classes are given to the trainees. They learn to crack safes and alarm systems. They're even taught about bombs on how to make them and disarm them if needed. Billy keeps at this training for several months. Then the Zeppelin reaches the old training island the Sky Pirates used.

Here the training gets to be more service, the trainees are pushed to the limit, so much so they're almost ready to quit. Billy takes them aside and explains why they're being trained. Each team will be sent to the specific island where one of the Five lives. The trainees needed to get in close to the particular target in hopes they can kidnap their mark, and bring them here. If one person on the team is taken out the rest of, you'll have to fill in the gap.

"Since none of you have any kind of criminal record, you should be able to get into where the person of the Five lives, wither by stealth or get appointed to be a guard," explains Billy.

"The woman can use their feminine wiles to get in close. Maybe to get information for the rest of the team, how far they chose to go with that is up to them." The Princess points out.

Billy continues his outline. "The women will be equipped with a series of drugs that'll render the man of the Five senseless to make it easy to spirit him away. I can't put a time table to this, that'll be determined by each team. Any questions?"

No one says anything. "Good, you'll need to keep this to your selves. I still need to pare the team down another ten people, and you have all made it difficult to choose. Take this night off, and the Princess and I will make our decisions by morning." states Billy.

The trainees leave. Leaving Billy and Vantessa alone. Billy turns to the Princess, "let's take a walk."

"Ok. Vantessa is puzzled; it's as if Billy is apprehensive about something.

They walked in for a mile into the wilderness of the island. Billy holds up his hand for Vantessa to be silent. Vantessa is looking at Billy in alarm. Billy grabs her and pulls her into the brush. They wait in the quiet, and one of the men from the crew is snaking upon them. Billy remains motionless, then springs upon the man and brings him down upon the ground.

"Why're you following us?" demands Billy.

"No reason, I was just out for a walk," said the crewman.

"I know you; you were one of the guards watching the Five's doubles," said the Princess.

"No, I'm not one of the guards," said the crewman.

"I know better." The Princess touches the man's neck, causing him to writhe in pain. Billy stands aside to watch.

"What did the men offer you?" demands the Princess.

"Nothing, I was just out for a walk, don't hurt me." Cries out the crewman.

The Princess touched the other side of his neck and let him writhe in more pain. The Princess turns away as if she didn't care. Before she takes two steps, Billy knocked her aside and killed the crewman, before he could kill the Princess.

"Billy, you didn't need to kill him," said Vantessa.

"Yes Vantessa, I did, if I hadn't, you'd be dead now." Billy picks up the knife the man had and showed it to her.

"He shouldn't have been able to move," Vantessa said.

Billy took out a flashlight and pulled the crewman's shirt off. On the crewman's arm the man had received a shot of a pain killer.

"Vantessa, he was play-acting to be in pain. So, he could get close to one of us."

"I think you're right; by the way, how did you know we were being followed?" asked Vantessa.

"I thought I saw something on the fringe after we told the trainees to break up. So, I lead him here. I wish we could've kept him alive; he could've given us more information."

"Why did you kill him, Billy? I have never seen you do that ever", whispers Vantessa.

"I was afraid for you, so I reacted. I realized that my life wouldn't be worth living without you."

"Do you love me, Billy?" asked Vantessa.

"Yes, I do. I have never loved anyone else. Enough of this now, we've work to do before we can explore this love, I have for you." stammers Billy.

Vantessa says nothing, but she smiles to herself. Then she realizes she feels the same way about Billy. Billy takes her aside, and they move away from the body. After a time, Billy leads the Princess back to the brig, where the guards they captured on the island were being kept. Billy singles one out and takes him down to another cell out of sight. Then he starts yelling at him; later, he puts the man in great pain with a nerve pinch. The man screams, and Billy continues to yell at the captured guard, then all goes quiet. The man is rendered unconscious with a nerve pinch.

"Guards come and take this dead body out of here and

bring me another prisoner," Billy shouts, so the other four men would believe the man was killed. The body is moved to another cell out of sight, and another man is brought in for questioning.

"I killed the first man because he wouldn't talk to me. I'm going to give you the same chance as I gave him now, will you answer my questions or do I do the same to you?"

The man is white with fear, and he is shaking.

"Wha... Wha... do you want to know?" The guard of the Five stammers.

"What country are you from, and I want the layout of the compound where your employer lives."

"I... I... can't he'll kill me if I tell you." stammers the man.

"Look I just killed the man before you, what makes you think I won't kill you?" says Billy in a stern voice.

"He's killing me will be terrible, you at least won't make it last; I'd rather die quickly at your hands." the man pleads.

Billy applies a nerve pinch to the man and lets him writhe in pain, and he squirms about screaming. Billy stops the pain, "are you going to tell me what I want to know or not?"

"No, please don't force me." screams the man.

Billys applies the nerve pinch and let the man writhe in pain longer.

"Now tell me what I want to know," says Billy.

"Ahh! I can't, please stop the pain." He pleads.

"No, I'll leave you in pain until you tell me what I want to know," said Billy.

The man screams and screams. Billy puts him out as if he had just killed him.

"Guards, take away the body, and bring me another one of the men," Billy said this loud enough so the last three men can hear him.

As the guards removed the body, they go to the cell and bring out another man; he starts gibbering as he is brought to the cell where Billy is waiting.

"Now tell me what I want to know, and you'll live. It's as simple as that", states Billy.

"What do you want to know?" the man gibbered.

"What country is your employer from, and I'd like the layout for his castle." Asked Billy in an off-handed way.

"He'll kill me!" gibbers the man.

"As you may have noticed, I just killed two of you. I take it you'd rather die now instead of later?" asked Billy.

"I'd rather not die at all." The man stammers.

"Then tell me what I want to know, and you can stay aboard my ship until this is all finished, one way or another. What do you say?" says Billy.

"Ok, I'll talk. What do you want to know?" He pleads.

"What large island nation are you from?" queries Billy.

"Wexford."

"Good, now here is some paper and now draw me a map to show me where the castle is. Then draw me a diagram of the castle its self, and show me all the strategic locations. Amory, his bedroom, and possible escape routes."

Chapter

31

The man makes the required sketches and hands them over to Billy. Billy accepts them and leads him to a new cell. Three down and two to go. Billy calls for the fourth man to be brought to him, like the last man he wants to live. So, extracting the requested information was less taxing. The last man is much more difficult. Billy uses all that he knows to bring the man pain without killing him. The man wouldn't break, so Billy calls in Vantessa so she can put on a show for the captive. A brazier is brought in, and all sorts of knives, and a medicine chest with all kinds of vials of colored liquid with needles of varying sizes and lengths.

The man is secured to a chair, and Vantessa puts on her show. The man turns pale as she brandished her hot poker before his eyes. She even touches the skin on his right arm, before he breaks down and begs to give up the information that is asked of him. After he complies, he's taken to a different cell.

"Well, Vantessa, are you ready to convince the other two

men to give up what we need from them?" asks Billy.

"I am; it's kind of fun playing bad cop to your good cop. Let's hope the men break as easily as this last one. In all honesty, I don't like to torture people, kill them yes, torture no." says Vantessa.

The next man is brought in, and Billy wakes him up.

"You didn't kill me!" Then he spits in Billy's face.

"No, I still want that information that you have," said Billy.

"You'll never get it from me," he screams.

"Too bad, Princess, you may do your worsted." Billy steps to one side to reveal all the tools and the like that are behind him. The Princess re-enters the room and goes for the hot poker.

"What are you doing, the man screams?"

"Well, you won't give me what I asked for in such a nice way, so the Princess here will ask you her way. While she's working on you, remember what your employer did to her family. So, she'll enjoy making you talk. Just remember I gave you a chance to tell me," said Billy.

"Can we talk about this?" begs the man.

"Are you going to give me the information I asked for?" queried Billy.

"Yes, I will." The man nearly sobs.

Billy has the man carted off to a cell where he can draw up the requested sketches.

Now on to the last man. Billy wakes up the last man, with the same effect as the one before him. Then the Princess enters and starts playing with the hot poker.

"Now, before I let the Princess work on you, will you not

give up the information I asked for?"

"No, where are the other men?" he asks.

"They died during questioning, two of them are now gibbering simpletons. The drugs she uses made them talk, and when it ran its course, they've no mind left. Would you like to see them?" asks Billy.

"I won't talk," said the last guard.

"Ok, Princess, do what you want to him," said Billy.

The Princess approaches the man with the hot poker and as she is moving it around his face. The man is calling her all kinds of profanity; the Princess keeps her head until he spits in her face. Then she lays the hot poker on the man's face. She was causing him to scream out in pain. Billy doesn't interfere with her. The Princess re-heats the poker so she can do more damage. Then Billy pulls her aside to talk to her.

"This man is not going to break, what if we inject him with a sedative and put him to sleep, then thank him when he wakes for the information. Then put all the men back into the same cell. I believe this will spark some conversation between them, and we may discover that the information we have gathered may be false. If not, we'll at least have four of the Five's layouts," said Billy.

"I'll go along with that Billy; my heart is not in this right now. I almost killed that man in there. I rather like your deception better than being the torcher," said Vantessa.

"Good, let's put him to sleep," said Billy

The Princess goes to her case, takes out a rather long syringe, pulls one of the colored vials, fills the needle, and approaches the man strapped to the chair.

"You; You witch! Stay away from me, no matter what you do, I'll not talk!" As the guard stains against his bonds.

The Princess sticks the long needle into the man's thigh and injects him. The whole time he squirms and shouts profanity at both Billy and the Princess. The drug finally takes effect. Billy has him moved back to the first cell, and then he instructs his men to put all the men back into the same cell and to listen carefully to see what they do. The guards are to listen to what the Five guards say when they're back to gather when the sedative wears off Billy is outside the cell looking in.

Billy addressed the last man, and thanks to him for providing the information he wanted in front of the other men. Then Billy leaves. The guards are just out of sight of the cell, and they listen to the conversation between the captured guards to see what they'd say.

An hour later, the guards came to Billy's office to report on what they've heard. As Billy suspected, most of the information the guards provided was false. Billy decides to follow his original plan to get his people into positions of security among the Five so they can get in on the inside to make their capture and spirit the men away from their castles. This will also have to be done on the same day or night. So that the Five don't hear about it and guard against the kidnappings.

That night Billy and Vantessa explain to the team what they're to do within the six-month time table they have to meet the objective. They set a date to pull this off and meet back up at the Zeppelin. Each team is sent off so they can fly to their destinations to begin their infiltration and capture. Each side makes it to the island country where the target is hold up. After a time, each person manages to get a position on the Five's guard. In time the Pirates distinguish themselves and get moved up into place, closer to their target. On the date designated, they pull off the kidnapping of each of the Five men and manage to capture their target. And get them loaded on to a plane and fly out to where the Zeppelin is waiting for them.

Billy has the actual Five men secured in different places on the Zeppelin, so they don't know they all have been kidnapped. Billy and Vantessa are the only ones to talk to the men. Billy decides that the Five guardsmen need to be put off the Zeppelin on to a remote island. They are no longer required. Then Billy communicates to his friend Bruiser at the secret police head quarters. Billy gives Bruiser a location where they can meet. Bruiser agrees to comply with Billy.

Chapter

32

"Oops! I see some droopy heads over there; it's time to stop recording and call it a night."

"AAH, grandpa, do we have to stop now?" complains Jeff.

"Looks like I'd better do just that you and your sister are falling asleep."

"It was getting interesting, grandpa," said Jeff.

"I know, but tomorrow is another day, and I need to get some sleep myself so I can collect my thoughts."

Jeff's dad and mom pick up the children and carry them into the house and up to bed.

"Dad, how much longer will this story take?" asks Doug.

"There is still quite a bit left, to tell about, why did you want to go home and come back next week?" asks Grandpa.

"No, Dad, I want to get the whole story, while you still have the details fresh in your mind."

"How about we start tomorrow early?"

"That'll be fine; by the way, you'll have had to stop anyway I need to load up another file to record on," said Doug.

"Good. See you all in the morning then. Good night." says, grandpa.

The morning seems to come very fast. Mom is up in the kitchen, making breakfast so they can get an early start on the story, with the dishes out of the way. Everyone with anticipation watches grandpa as he gets ready to dazzle the family with his story.

"Grandpa, how did the Five get kidnapped?" asks Jeff.

"Well, Jeff, there's a lot of speculation about that and rumors. But when you get down to it, the only people who know are the ones who did the kidnapping. I guess that'd make a good story as well. At this time, it's a moot point. Billy and Vantessa have captured the Five and are trying to decide what to do with them." Grandpa now launches off into his story.

Several days later, Billy leaves the Zeppelin in his plane and flies to the island where the Queen ruled the Sky Pirates from to meet up with Bruiser for a pow-wow about the Five. Billy gets to the island before Bruiser and lands his plane, then Billy taxis his aircraft to the far end of the field where the trees and brush are the thickest. Billy pushes his plane into the brush and covers it up in case he needs to leave undetected.

Bruiser arrives the next day and lands on the runway and then taxis his plane into a hangar; later, he builds a fire to signal Billy all is clear. Billy shows up that night from out of the dark.

"So old friend, you managed to get here," said Billy, which makes Bruise jump with a start.

"Hi, Billy, I should've known that you'd already be here."

"I was, I watched you and the sky for several hours, to make sure you came alone."

"I came as I said I would. But I suspect we don't have long before the force that followed me will soon arrive", said Bruiser.

"Ok, I have the Five. Where and when can I turn them over to you for trial?" asks Billy

"You can't. If you give them to me, I'd have to release them. Even with the evidence, you provided me. In most normal cases, I could arrest them. But the Five control the whole planet. They would be released based on that alone." complained Bruiser.

"What, but the evidence that I have on them!?" mutters Billy.

"As I said, Billy, I'd have to let them go. They've too much power in government and within the law enforcement. There is nothing I can do, I'm sorry," said Bruiser

"I guess that says it all, Bruiser."

"I'm afraid so, Billy. I've orders to bring you in and your gang as well. If you leave, now I can say you got away before I got here."

"Thanks, Bruiser." Billy gets up and walks off into the dark.

"Don't get caught, Billy, any of you. It'll be a death sentence if you do," shouts Bruiser.

Billy doesn't answer. Billy soon makes it to his plane, where he uncovers it to make preparations to leave when he hears several plans coming in for a landing. Billy realizes he cannot take off now. He'll have to wait. Soon ten planes land on the field, and Bruiser has them park in the hangar with his aircraft, and he uses the excuse of hiding the planes from sight. Then Bruiser leads the men to the castle to start a search for Billy.

To keep with regulations, Bruiser leaves one-armed man behind to guard the planes. Billy has been watching the whole time and realizes what a friend Bruiser is. Billy sneaks up on guard, and soon renders him asleep without so much as a whimper. Billy returns to his plane, and finishes clearing off the brush, and soon is taxing down the runway, bringing several of Bruiser's men to investigate the noise. They soon find the man Billy has knocked out. One or two of the men get into their planes to give chase when Bruiser stops them.

"Sir, he is getting away." shouts a crewman.

"Very true, but did you check your plane over to make sure he didn't sabotage the one you're flying?" asks Bruiser.

"No, Sir."

"Then you might want to make sure of your plane, or did you forget that Billy Webber knows how to work on planes and would know how to sabotage them."

The man turns pale, "I get your point, sir!"

That night the men turn in. And in the light of the morning, they find that none of the planes had been tinkered with.

"Sir, we could've given chase to this Pirate Billy Webber after all."

"Yes, we could've. On the other hand, Billy could've sabotaged several planes and killed several of us. Did you want to chance that in the dark?" asks Bruiser.

"No, Sir."

"Now mount up and let's head in the direction we heard

him leaving in and see if we can spread out to find him," commands Bruiser.

"Yes, Sir."

The men board their planes, fly off the island, and head towards the mainland in line with each man spreading apart, hoping they'll spot Billy's plane. Bruiser and his men didn't know that Billy has circled and lands back on the island after they all leave. Figuring that Bruiser would follow procedure and do what he just did. Billy contacts Vantessa and tells her that the island is clear for now and that they can land the Zeppelin.

Chapter

33

The next morning the Zeppelin drops down out of the clouds and lands at the landing strip where Billy is waiting; after they loaded up his plane, they're ready to take off, but Vantessa decides they should spend the day. There were a few things she wants. She wants to see if they are still there in the castle. Billy knows better but gives in to her request. Billy goes with her and tells the men to get the Zeppelin ready for liftoff, and if any planes should return, the crew should ascend without them. When Billy and the Princess reach the castle, Billy hears planes approaching. Billy calls the Zeppelin and tells them to get out of there, and he and the Princess will hide in the castle until they can get-away.

The Zeppelin ascends and just gets out of sight in the cloud cover above when Bruiser and his squadron returned to the island.

"Alright, you, goldbricking troops, spread out and search this island Billy is here somewhere," commands Bruiser.

The squad spreads out and searches the hangars, and

works their way to the castle.

"I suspected Bruiser would do this. That's why I kept the Zeppelin ready to leave. Vantessa, do you have any hideaways here where we can wait out the search?" asks Billy.

"I think so, Billy, follow me."

Vantessa leads them to a blank wall on the main floor, and she probes the molding along the wall until she finds a switch. Then she presses it, and it opens the wall just wide enough to admit one person at a time. They squeeze into the passageway, and Vantessa closes the opening. As it turns out, it's just in the nick of time one of the troopers has just entered the very room where Billy and Vantessa just left.

Vantessa leads Billy down a long corridor and into a dead-end room with a bed in it.

"We'll be safe here, Billy, as long as they don't find the hidden switch," says Vantessa.

The light is filtering in from a window overlooking the courtyard. "Quite a cozy place with one bed here, Vantessa."

"We used this room to hide certain guests when we did not want other people to know they were on the island; now it'll do to hide us for a short time," said Vantessa.

Billy looks out the window and sees that most, if not all, of Bruiser's squadron, are searching every nook and cranny looking for him.

"Vantessa is there another way out of this dead-end, other than the way we came in?" asks Billy.

"No, this is the only place I could think of on such short notice," mentions Vantessa.

"OK, that may work just the same. Is there a way to see

who's in the room we left before we open the door from this side?" queries Billy.

"Yes, there is a peephole," said Vantessa.

"OK, good, let's wait, and see how resolved they are in looking for me." Billy stretches and looks at Vantessa, "I need to get some sleep. I'll curl up on the floor here next to the bed and try to get some much-needed sleep." Yawns Billy.

"Why not use the bed?" Vantessa asks.

"You may want to get some rest yourself, Vantessa, and we both cannot use the bed."

"Still afraid of me, are you!" she asks.

"I'm not afraid of you; I'm afraid of myself in your presents." Billy rolls over and tries to fall asleep.

"You know you don't need to be worried about how you feel about me because I love you too, Billy. You know that, right?" whispers Vantessa.

"I know that. That makes me even more fearful." Billy curls up next to the bed, and Vantessa sits looking at him with a strange look on her face. Of all the men, Vantessa has known. They've all tried at one time or another to bed her. And now she has fallen for a man who'll not take advantage of her. Even when she welcomes it, Vantessa smiles as she hears him breathe slowly, then takes the heaver blanket from the bed and covers Billy over.

Under her breath, she says, "Billy, my love, you're the most remarkable man I've ever met. I hope we can live through this trial; I'd like to be your wife."

Vantessa stands up and carefully peers out the window to watch the activity just below them in the courtyard. After a time, she lays down and falls asleep. What seems like only a few minutes, Billy wakes her up. Then he puts his hand over her mouth and whispers.

"Don't say anything; someone is in the hidden passageway," whispers Billy.

Billy has her to get under the bed, and he puts the blanket back on the bed. Then he stands to one side to wait. Soon one of Bruiser's men shuffles into the room. Before he can raise the alarm, Billy puts him to sleep with his neck pinch. Then Billy moves down the passage to the hidden door and then comes rushing back to get Vantessa.

Billy whispers, "we have to get out of here."

They reach the hidden door, and Vantessa stops him; then goes over to a place on the wall and looks out the peephole and sees no one in the room. Once out in the room, Vantessa takes the lead; and she heads them into a passage that'll take them to cave underneath the castle.

"Vantessa Bruiser knows of the cave, he and I found it. whispered Billy."

"I know; we'll stop before we get there to check it out to ensure there is no one there. If we can get there, we can use the other passage to get out and maybe find a plane we can take to escape."

"Lead on, Vantessa."

Vantessa leads the way through twisting and winding corridors, and stairs are heading downward when she comes to a dead-end Vantessa starts feeling along with the molding on the blank wall's inner corner. Billy hears people in the corridor coming their way.

"Vantessa hurry, we've company coming," whispers Billy.

"I'm trying to remember; it's been a while." Vantessa continues to look, and she finds it, then she presses the button. The wall swings inward, and they rush into the dark and try to push the wall closed. Just as its creeps closed, one of the crewmen sees it moving, but he's not sure.

"Sir, that wall just closed, I'm sure of it."

Bruiser looks him in the eye for a few moments. "OK, that means there is a switch here somewhere you find it. The rest of you continue searching. I want Billy Webber captured alive."

The rest of the men backtrack, leaving the trooper who saw the wall close and Bruiser, they're looking for the switch that'll open the wall. Bruiser is beside himself; Billy is a good friend. But Bruiser has to catch him Before someone else does. Billy and Vantessa are wanted DEAD or ALIVE. Bruiser wants them alive.

As Bruiser and the trooper keep searching, Billy and Vantessa escape down into the caves below the castle. As they reach the floor Vantessa pulls Billy into an adjoining cave, she finds the notch in the wall and reaches in to pull out a small bag, that she had hidden there a long ago. It has a huge diamond in it. The diamond is as big as her hand.

"Hey Vantessa, we have plenty of money aboard the Zeppelin, why do we need this one?"

"To getaway, we can use it as bait to slow them down," suggest Vantessa.

"OK, where to? You know this place better than I do," said Billy.

"This way." Vantessa takes them down to the mouth of the cave, where the water is just now going out with the tide.

"Billy, they'll find the latch soon and be on us soon. We'll have to swim for it," said Vantessa.

Billy and the Princess dive into the water, using the current to be swept out from the cave into the open water where they swim to a cove not far from the cave entrance. They climb out on to the beach. and move up into the brush to hide and see who or what might be around them.

Bruiser and the trooper move through the open wall and jump down into the cave. As they approach the floor of the cave, Bruiser believes he hears water splashing, and he runs to the cave entrance. Bruiser does not see anyone, maybe he just thought he did, so he and the trooper search the cave. Find nothing; they return up into the castle.

Billy and Vantessa make their way through the woods heading back to the landing strip to see what chance they might have in stealing one of the secret police planes. At the edge of the runway across from the hangars, Billy and Vantessa hunker down to watch for sentries. They sit there for an hour and see no one. They decide to break cover and run to the nearest plane, then stop when from out of nowhere Five sentries show up with drawn guns.

Billy and Vantessa hunker back down in the brush to watch. The men split up and spread out to cover all of the planes.

"That doesn't look good," whispers Vantessa.

Billy nods to her in assent. Billy isn't sure what to do. If Bruiser calls in more troops, he realizes they'll be caught. Billy grabs Vantessa's arm and leads her away from the landing strip back into the brush to talk with her about what he has in mind in obtaining transportation.

"Princess, we're not both going to get out of this. I can convince Bruiser that I'm here alone, and when they take me in you can get away", says Billy

"NO! I'll not leave you!" states Vantessa.

"I'm not finished; when you get away, you can recruit the people we trained to break me out of jail. Or at the least trade me for the Five." reasons Billy.

"No! I don't like it; they may kill you before I can make arrangements," says Vantessa.

"We may have to chance that. If Bruiser is down there, I may not be killed. He wants me alive; that is why he's here to capture me." states Billy.

"Then I'll go with you too," she demands.

"You know that is not going to work. That diamond that you have; let me have it; I have an idea. If they think I know where more treasure is, it may make them sloppy. No one likes to lose a fortune, or they may fight over it. Keep your eyes on me. If this works, I'll be back for you."

She hands over the diamond, and Billy takes off into the brush and moves to the far end of the landing strip. Billy breaks cover and stands up in the plain sight of the sentry. With his hands raised and the big diamond well displayed in his left hand.

The sentry sees him and holds his gun on him.

"You! Come over here where I can see you!" commands the sentry.

Billy walks over to where the sentry is with his hands raised.

The sentry is on his guard. But hasn't yet shouted to the others, "what do you have in your hand?" the sentry asks.

"Just this diamond, nothing else," said Billy.

The sentry is curious, "Show it to me!"

"I'll have to lower one of my hands, is that alright?"

"As long as you do it slowly." states the sentry. The sentry comes within two arm lengths of Billy, and his gun is centered on Billy's chest. "Now throw the diamond to me carefully."

While Billy is trying to get arrested, Vantessa follows him and stays to the shadows, then when the sentry and Billy's attention is centered on each other Vantessa moves around both of them and comes up behind the sentry. As Billy pitches the diamond to the sentry, Vantessa strikes with accuracy and knocks the man out then relieves him of his gun.

"Now get in that plane and get us out of here!" yells Vantessa.

Billy climbs up into the pilot's seat, followed by Vantessa. They strap in, and Billy fires up the plane and pulls out on to the taxiway and then crosses over to the runway. Turning into the wind, Billy pushes the power throttles full forward. The plane moves down the runway picking up speed. From the hangar area, the plane is hit several times from gunfire. Vantessa returns fire in hopes everyone ducks and gives them a chance to get off the runway. One of the bullets fired at them hits Vantessa in the right shoulder, but she says nothing as Billy launches into the air and heads for the low cloud cover. Soon on their heels, a few of the other Secret Police; man, their planes to give chase. Soon two planes are hot on Billy and Vantessa's trail.

Vantessa soon passes out in the rear cockpit; she had put her belt on knowing Billy might have to do some fancy flying to get away from their pursuers. Once in the cloud cover, Billy changes direction to head back over the island and to try to meet up with the Zeppelin hovering at ten thousand feet. Billy makes a call to the ship using a code because the Secret Police will be listening in. Billy can't see Vantessa in the back seat and isn't aware she's injured. The hangar section on the Zeppelin opens, and Billy flies into it and lands in the hangar. As soon as Billy touches down, the Zeppelin heads further out to sea. Billy hops down and turns to help Vantessa, but she's not moving. Billy crawls back up to a section of the cockpit and sees her passed out and blood everywhere. Billy turns a few shades pale, for fear she may be dead.

She moans, and everyone hurries to take her to sickbay to be treated. They soon find that she'll be alright, the bullet missed any vital organs, but she lost a lot of blood. Under the care of trusted people, Vantessa comes around. When she opens her eyes, she sees Billy next to her bed with her hand in his. He smiles at her, then holds her down as she tries to sit up.

"The medic says you are going to be OK, but you need to rest Vantessa," said Billy in a quiet voice.

"What happened?" she asks.

"You were shot. When I landed and got out, I saw all that blood and was scared you were dead. Now you need to be resting so you'll heal. I'll be nearby, so if you need anything, just call me," said Billy.

Vantessa holds his hand and soon falls back to sleep. Billy

sits there almost crying; he's terrified that he could've gotten her killed. That's not going to happen again! Billy seems to almost die inside when he saw all her blood in the cockpit. Now that he's right here watching her, Billy realizes that he couldn't live without Vantessa. Then and there, Billy decides to marry her if she'll have him. It takes a better part of a week for Vantessa to recover enough that she is allowed to return to her quarters, and Billy is always within shouting distance of her. Vantessa rather likes the fact that Billy is still close at hand to her.

Billy still has a perplexing problem of the Five. What to do with them? It's not in his nature to kill people. Then he decides that he could desert them on an island where they may or may not be found. If the Five were out of circulation for a significant period. The world might change for the better. That evening Billy tells Vantessa what he plans to do to the Five. She disagrees with him. In her mind, they should die for all they have done to her family and others. Over time, Billy wins out when he points out that the Five will have to work with their own hands to survive. After all, it's decided; Billy tries to locate an island outside standard travel lanes and has sufficient size to find food and shelter.

After an extensive search, Billy manages to find an island that will suit his needs, two days later Billy herds the Five off the Zeppelin on to the open beach.

"According to my men, this island has all you need to live. To the North, you'll find a cliff wall where you can build a home of sorts. In a pile over there are tools for you to use. There is sufficient animal life and fish to sustain you." said

Billy

"You can't do this, said one of the Five."

"Watch me!" said Billy.

"Take us back. We'll pay you anything," said another of the Five.

"No! this is your punishment for all you've done to the people of this world. You make me sick. All the deaths that you caused so you can be rich. Living off other people's troubles. I could've killed you and left your bodies here. I think this is a better way to pay you back. A prison without release." Billy states sternly.

Billy climbs back on to the Zeppelin, and it soon lefts, leaving the Five men on the island. As it turns out, they were never found. Billy and his men (Sky Pirates) were blamed for the Five's deaths. The world did start moving in a better direction from a dictatorship to a worldwide republic. The only person to know that Billy did the world a favor is Bruiser. Even though he'd have to arrest Billy and Vantessa if he crossed their path, he knew they made the world a better place.

Chapter

34

That's not the end of the story; the next part is what I heard but cannot verify. Anyway, Billy and the Princess got married and tried to figure out a way to disband the Sky Pirates so that none of them would get caught by the law. Some of them returned home, and others took up residence in some of the outlying islands. Billy sets the Zeppelin adrift. The Secret Police find it and board it to find no one aboard. They surmise it belonged to the Sky Pirates. Billy and Vantessa return to Billy's hangar; to stay for a short time; as a matter of fact, I got to meet Mrs. Billy Webber, and she was a beauty, and full of fire. She loved Billy to distraction. Billy couldn't go anywhere or do anything without her being there. Even some times being underfoot, and Billy wouldn't have it any other way.

One day several months later, Vantessa tells Billy she needs to go to the doctor's office. Billy offers to take her, and she said no! That she will be just fine. Vantessa goes to the doctor, and he tells Vantessa is going to have a child. Vantessa glows so much she seems ever prettier than before. That night at dinner, Vantessa tells Billy he is going to be a father.

"I'm going to be a father!" stammers Billy.

"Yes, we're going to be parents," states Vantessa.

Billy almost passes out, "I'm going to be a father!"

"Men! Says Vantessa, and she laughs, and it sounds musical.

Life seems to be going well; they're not being pursued as they have been. Billy and Vantessa live their lives as a married couple, with their first child on its way. The frequent trips to the doctor manages to draw attention to Vantessa; even though they have been living a quiet life, it seems someone recognized the Princess from a wanted poster. She'd be delivering her first child in a few more months, on her latest trip to the doctor, she is followed back to Billy's hangar.

After Vantessa returns to their home, she sees the two men who are following her. She escapes using the back of the hangar and finds Billy at his friend's hangar where he's working on a plane.

"Billy, I've been found out, and two men are watching the hangar where we live. What are we going to do?" asks Vantessa.

Billy wipes his hands off and hugs his wife, "We better leave before we get Jim Collens and his family involved." Billy walks up to the side door, and spy's the two men. He gathers Vantessa and heads home using the back way to the hangar. Billy grabs the backpacks; he has made ready for just this need. He and Vantessa return to his hangar. Billy loads them onto the plane. Then he put his wife in the back seat and has her to strap in. Billy opens his hangar doors and rushes to his aircraft and fires it up. The policemen in the car. Realize that something is about to happen, so they get out of the car and rush to the hangar.

By the time the men get their Billy has cleared the doors and is speeding down the taxiway to the landing strip so he can take off. Billy throttles up his plane, the men fire on the plane but miss. Billy is soon in the air heading for the crystal canyon. The two men hurry back to the car to call in that Billy Webber, and the Princess are escaping in a plane.

"Wife, do you trust me?" asks Billy.

"With my life, Billy."

"We are going to the crystal canyon, and soon we'll be surrounded by the secret police."

"Do what you must, Billy, I don't want to be captured and put in prison."

"If what I have discovered is true, we'll not be captured; however, we'll disappear just like all the other people before us who went to the canyon."

"What do you mean, Billy?"

"The crystal canyon has swallowed up everyone whoever enters it. Whether they fly or hike in."

"What about the baby, Billy?"

"The child will be with us wherever we go; wife, I will not let anything happen to you."

As Billy flies over the field, Jim watches him go knowing he'll never see Billy again. Billy and Vantessa are soon surrounded by the planes of the Secret Police, and they try to force Billy to land his aircraft. The Secret Police have forgotten that Billy is one of the best racers of his time and that he's the only person in the world who threaded the stone needle, and lived to tell about it.

Billy leads the Secret Police into the canyon, where he once again threads the stone needle losing most of the planes on his tail. Then Billy drops down deep into the canyon and flies on until he reaches the crystal canyon and all the aircraft that are following dropped back, knowing what has happened to others who've entered the canyon. Billy was never heard from again. All I can hope for is that he and the Princess are living a full life somewhere else. That is the whole story as I know it.

"Grandpa, where did Billy and the Princess go?"

"Well Jeff no one knows, but because Billy removed the Five from our lives, this became a better world and Bruiser Billy's friend found the evidence on the men and had it published so that if the men do turn up, they'll spend the rest of their lives in prison."

"Son, that's all the story I know about Billy Webber. I'd give anything to know how he is doing or if he is alive. I guess we'll never know."

"Dad, Thanks for the story. I've got it all recorded. I'll archive it into the library system for others to hear."

"Thanks, Son, I think Billy would like that."

The next day the Collins family packs up and says goodbye to grandpa and thank him for his story, and they depart to return home. As they leave, grandpa stands there watching them as they disappear into the distance. "I hope you're doing well. My friend." Jim turns to go back into his house.

Epilog

Billy and Vantessa are nearly blinded by the bright light reflecting from the crystal as they passed through the crystal canyon. Billy manages to keep his plane level until they passed through it. Then all they can see is desert in all directions, a sea of sand as far as the eye can see. Billy takes the plane up higher and still only sees sand, and the heat is oppressive. Vantessa passes out in the back but is still breathing. Billy flies on in hopes of finding a good place to land his plane.

After hours of flying, Billy sees a small green area, miles ahead, and so Billy flies towards it and when he arrives. Billy circles the place and sees a village on one side with people in it. Billy decides to land to see if he can get some information about the area. Billy sets his aircraft down, and when it is shut down, he reaches under the dash and pulls a component out of its place and puts it into his pocket. Billy hops out of the plane and checks on Vantessa and gently wakes her up.

"Honey, are you ok?" asks Billy in a concerned voice.

She smiles and nods; at that moment, Billy is pulled from the plane and thrown down on to the ground. Billy jumps up and confronts the man who manhandled him.

"What are you doing?" demands Billy.

"I'm taking your property; what did you think I'm doing?"

the man blusters.

"I don't think so!" said Billy with defiance.

The man pulls a knife, "And you are going to stop me, Big man?"

Billy approaches the big man as the man slashes downward with his knife. Billy brushes aside the man's arm and jabs him in the armpit, causing that arm to go numb, and the man drops the knife. The man takes a swing with a haymaker with his other arm out of desperation at Billy's head. Again, Billy ducks under the swing and hits the man in the other armpit causing both arms to go numb. The man takes one look at Billy and runs away. Billy returns to the cockpit to check on Vantessa.

Billy helps Vantessa out of the plane, and they walk up to the gate of the village, and it's opened as they enter, and a man with a spear confronts them.

"What do you want here?" he says gruffly.

"To get food and water, and a place to rest for a day or so," said Billy

The guard points over to a corner building "You can find what you asked for over there."

Billy is looking around and sees that the whole place is more or less a pigsty. Animal dung everywhere you look. You could catch fleas or lice form a person just passing by them. Billy takes Vantessa into the building and shedders from the filth. A man approaches, "What do you want?"

"I'm looking for a place for my wife to lie down and some clean water and food to eat," said Billy

"How much money do you have; this is not a charity here,

you know."

Billy takes out a silver coin and tosses it to the man, "what will that buy?" asks Billy

The man bites down on the coin and says, "It'll do." The man points to the stairs; it's the first room you come to. Billy assists his wife up the stairs to their room.

Billy has landed on a new world full of sand. His adventures will continue in this new world.

The End.